THE GRAND MARKET

It was a hot summer day in the city state of Ebb. The sun's light shone brightly upon the cube shaped marble buildings that sprawled from the southern ocean shore into the surrounding wasteland. In the center of the town was a large rock spire that rose a mile out of the ground. The spire had been painstakingly carved into an even oval shaped cylinder with several openings to accommodate the sky ships that were zipping in and out. The city had declared the spire as the first sky dock, and the people had affectionately named the column the Grand Market. Within the Grand Market, the ship captains would pick up or discard crew members at any of the local boarding houses that had been built just beyond the dock. Along the streets built within the column were a mixture of temporary and permanent buildings that belonged to travelers and settlers. The temporary market thrived from the wares of travelling merchants that had unloaded their goods from across the sea where Ebb had no conflicts, and the people of Ebb were the primary target for the goods sold. The permanent market was designed to only hold the inventory that was ordered from the captains and crew, and the show floor was a library of the catalogs for different shops throughout Ebb. A captain would place the order through a distributor and come back for the wares later.

Surrounding the Grand Market was a small ring of buildings, five buildings deep, that stood half the height of the column. This was the Inner Ring, also known as the Market District, and was littered with skyways that connected all the buildings with footpaths on multiple floors. An Ebbian could start from the Grand Market, and walk the entire perimeter of the Inner Ring without ever having to reach the ground level. The people of the Market District were mostly composed of the shop owners and workers, and these people were the landlords for most of Ebb and had a combined influence over the majority of the city state region of Ebb. The Inner Ring was also the home to the Grand Trial House were the elected representatives, known as the Judges, passed the laws and oversaw judicial matters. A child born within the Inner Ring was likely to grow up in luxury and become a merchant, Judge, or an officer in the Ebb Armed Forces, or the EAF.

Beyond the Inner Ring was the Second Ring, or the Industrial District, with buildings that stood three floors at the highest but was mostly composed of single story buildings. The people of the Industrial District tended to remain within their own ring with the exception of the market peddlers that brought the goods of the world to the Second Ring. Their carts would travel between the first two rings frequently to purchase the goods that were produced within the Second Ring and trade it off to the sky ships and buyers in the Grand Market. The people of the Second Ring tended to rent their buildings from the merchant lords of the Inner Ring and made deals with merchants to have their catalogs displayed. A child born within this district was likely to grow up working in one of the craft shops and would be a skilled worker by adulthood. Those children whose hearts screamed for adventure would sign up to be specialists within the EAF, such as crew members on warships or navigation experts within a Unit.

In the Industrial District, a traveler could purchase any crafted material from horseshoes and windows to the wondrous sky ship parts and the mysterious gears. It was within this ring, hundreds of years in the past, which the gears were first built and humanity first learned to utilize machinery for almost magical purposes. These metal objects had to be built of steel to work correctly, but the process to make a gear caused the steel to yellow and gain a grained appearance like bark on a tree. The first gear was the lift gear, which could be used to lift objects that weighed less than a hundred pounds and could stop projectiles within five yards of the wearer. This technology had risen alongside the use of gunpowder and had rendered the latter useless in a combat situation. Ebb expanded the construction of gears to produce several variant models that could produce fire or lightning, depending upon the power of the user, assist in the natural athleticism of the wearer, allow the wearer to breathe water, and even allow the operator to survive extreme temperatures. It was not long after the creation of the war gears that the gearsmiths of Ebb began to perfect their art and created the first gear mail, armors that incorporated several gears together. Ebb used the gear mail during its founding to take control of the southern eastern quarter of the Northern Continent, giving rise to the city state status. The Nenvian people of the north challenged Ebb in the war front and, with the combined effort of the Vagrant clans to the west of Ebb, stalled Ebb's effort for complete control of the Northern Continent. The war between Ebb and Nenva was settled in an armistice, and skirmishes still happen along the border between the two city states.

The Outer Ring of Ebb, otherwise known as the Poor District, has been expanded as a result of the war and the border conflicts. The people from the outskirts of the city state travel to the capital in hopes of rebuilding their broken lives but often find themselves stuck amongst the decrepit buildings and makeshift housing built of three walls and a curtain with tarp rooftops. Unlike the organized grid of streets and roads in the walled section of Ebb, the walkways in the Poor District are composed of winding passages the contain loops and curls and parts of the path are blocked off due to an unconventional placement of a random person's house. While poor in anything monetary, the people of the Outer Ring consider themselves rich in the arts, and indeed some of the finest painters and musicians will win the heart of some merchant lord and become a display amongst the Grand Market. The people in the district jokingly stated the only way out of the district was to become a famous artist or join the foot soldiers of the EAF, but the poor dreamed of learning the crafts of the Second Ring and gaining the wealth of the Inner Ring.

One such dreamer was a man by the name of Matthew Flint, and he dreamed of owning a sky ship and travelling the world. As a boy, Matthew had been a wiry street urchin dressed in overalls and little else. His dirty blonde hair was often coated in grease or mud and was just below his ears in length. Malnutrition had given his brown eyes a sunken look that carried on into adulthood, but his ambitions were as high as his spirits and a smile was constantly on his face. As a man, Matthew had thickened up from working as a carrier for the merchants, a profession he had changed as he aged. His hair had brightened from exposure to the sun, which his coworkers claimed he stole from everyone else due to being a head taller than most the other men. His smile had remained, but his choice in clothes had changed. Matthew's collection of clothes had been sold or traded for from the inter ring merchants and were made of fine silks for the shirts and durable denim for the pants. His large black boots complimented his long leather coat, and he topped his entire outfit with a feathered hat. Today, Matthew stood on an overturned crate in a back alley before a crowd of filthy men and women. Today, Matthew spoke of raiding in front of a thousand angry members of the Outer Ring.

"We all know the plan, but it pays to review it once more." Matthew spoke in a soft yet commanding tone. He had to motivate. "As soon as the day turns we slip into the breach in the wall. We don't want the guards to catch on, so we will be going in groups of five. Take a good look at the four people with you. Know their faces and names. These people will be your unit and your responsibility. Earlier today we made armbands for this mission. If your armband is red, you are an arson. Focus on the residential area to draw the attention of the guards and then proceed to the rendezvous point at the far end of the Second Ring. If your armband is blue, you are a supplier. Prioritize food and gears and don't kill unless you need to. We don't want to draw any extra attention to the plan. The rest of you should have green armbands. That means you are with me and are soldiers. Our job is to ambush the guards at the armory after the fire starts and collect as many weapons as we can. Then we rendezvous at the Inner Gate and make a rush for the *Daisy* and fly to freedom. Today we awoke as poor citizens of Ebb, but we will fall asleep as free pirates of the world." His broad smile was met with a small clamor of approval from the crowd before him. All of them eagerly watched as the sun began to set, ready to enact their plan. All of them except for one.

Alder Node was an old gear smith from the Second Ring. His bald head was covered this night by a short cap, and his eyes were still as a blue pond. He scratched the stubble on his face as he slipped away from the crowd in the street, leaving his armband in one of the nearby trash bins. Rumors of dissonance always come from the Poor District, but the rumors about the raid tonight had Alder concerned enough to investigate for himself. He had infiltrated the band easily enough by spotting the armbands that were being worn by hundreds of people. Though he was well into his sixties, Alder was a stout man from a lifetime of smithing and light on his feet due to his lift gear. Alder had ambushed one of the conspirators and took any identifying marks he might need. Slipping away had been simple as well, due to Alder's short stature making him hardly noticeable within a crowd. Once out of sight, Alder broke into a run to make it to the Second Ring in time to alert the guards of what was about to pass and to return to his shop to protect it and his apprentice. His approach to the Second Ring was halted at the gate, as a young guard looked questioningly upon the old man.

"Halt! It is already past the closing hour for the gates, so I cannot let you pass." The guard's words were measured and rehearsed. He was familiar with Outer Ring riffraff trying to sneak into the Second Ring.

"I'm Alder Node. This is my identification. I live in the Second Ring. Take me to your captain." Alder's voice was deep and pointed. He had never been the type to mince words. The guard looked over the identification papers that was handed to him before proceeding, while Alder tapped his foot impatiently. "Today, boy. There is an emergency."

"Nothing is more urgent than keeping the peace and keeping proper paperwork."

"I'm trying to keep the peace, boy! That's why I'm here!" Alder's voice began to rise from frustration.

"Settle down, Mr. Node. There is no reason for you to get yourself arrested tonight for disturbing the peace." The guard's patience was also expiring.

"Settle down? Settle down! There's gonna be fire tonight, boy! My shop, my home, my work is in danger and you are stalling me from getting there."

"Fire, eh? Well, your paperwork checks out, and I'll give your report of fire to the captain, but I'm going to have to ask you to move along." The guard opened the gate for Alder but made no move to find the captain.

"Steady your conscience, boy. This is a bad night to give half effort, and you'll be sore about it in the morning." Alder gave a grim tone to the guard as he passed and rushed for his own home.

The streets were deathly quiet in the Second Ring. Most of the shops were in the process of closing, and the hired help was heading for a long sleep. The Second Ring shops were preparing for the Festival of the Hunt which was taking place in the morning. The festival had originated as a means of redistribution of food to the populace after the fall harvest and to encourage the people to trim and clean the large amount of dead animals that had been brought into the city. The animals would be processed, and the city folk would be paid in meat and coin. It was a tradition far older than Ebb and had evolved with the city into a merchant party of cheap wares and gaudy masks. As the sun set, Alder passed several buildings that had already placed out deer head masks and bear pelt curtains in celebration for the festivities before arriving at his own two story shop. He was greeted by a stuffed giant scorpion pinned to the wall with a bowl of candy where the stinger used to be that must have been put up by his apprentice while he was away. The old man let out a sigh in sorrow and went inside to prepare for the raiders.

The shop was mostly the way Alder had left it. There were a few more lift gears and fire gears on the shelf, no doubt built by a bored apprentice. Most of his shop displayed the small home use gears and catalogs, but the far wall held his current trophy job, a set of gear mail designed with large wings. The torso was an interwoven mesh of small metal plates, designed to accommodate any wearer of sufficient enough size with sturdy rod shaped poles acting as a spine for the suit. On the back, the wings were made of intricately carved metallic feathers that were sharpened on one side and flattened on the other. There were each a small knife and were capable of making a full rotation if needed. The wings could serve as a blade or club, depending upon the intent of the wearer. Though the gear mail had a powerful lift system attached, Alder knew the suit would likely never fly because of the weight. This type of armor had been named wing mail and was usually made by sky ship captains. Alder's suit had been ordered a year prior and had been finished today. The file used to etch out the details was still lying beside the armor, and the smell of seasonings, fish, and potatoes was just now emerging from the upstairs apartment where the old master lived with his apprentice. She must have finished the final etchings within the hour. Alder followed his nose up the stairs to alert his apprentice.

The stairs led to a small box of a hallway with three doors. The left door was his own private space where he kept a couple of chairs for lounging and a small bed in the corner of the room for sleeping. It was a simple room that fulfilled its purpose and did no more. The right door led to his apprentice's room. Throughout Alder's life, the room had changed in furnishings and wall coverings five times, but the last change had lasted fifteen years and was occupied for the last five. The little girl had started as his apprentice when she was seven years old and had passed her gear smith test on her seventeenth birthday, the first day she was legally allowed to take the test. She was a prodigy of gears and would have been an officer in the military if she had been born in the Inner Ring. Alder had moved the young woman into his apprentice room with plans of teaching her his own secret crafting techniques. The old smith intended to retire when she was trained and announce her as his successor. A few more years and she would be ready, and Alder would be damned if he was going to let some hooligans from the Outer Ring destroy his fifteen year commitment to the training of this girl. Alder opened the door to the middle room, which led to the shared living space. Inside the living space was a small brown sofa with two cushions that sat beside a stack of newspapers that had been pushed into the corner. The floor was the same wooden boards that went throughout the building, but this room had a comfortable rug with a mixture of yellow chevrons and brown hoops that patterned across the entire room. On the far end was a standing stove beside a couple of metal pantries, and a red headed woman standing over a deep frying pan that was ready to overflow from its contents. The woman was Marla Thatch. Her fair skin was freckled with spots of light brown that ran across the entirety of her thin frame. Her hair was cut short on the sides and in the back, and the top was kept at her shoulders and was usually worn back in a tiny ponytail while she worked but had been left down today. She was dressed in a long white shirt and a pair of tight fitting brown pants that ended just above her bare feet. The outfit was completed with a light red apron that was used for cooking and was stained with the proof of its purpose. Her dark, forest green eyes darted across the meal she was preparing, directing her lift gear to prevent the food from spilling or burning while she hummed an upbeat tune. Her body moved in a light dance to the rhythm of her own song. Alder considered the consequences of not informing her of the upcoming raiders and handling the situation himself, but the thought of her fiery temper turning on him broke his heart, and he yielded to reason.

"Marla. We've got a problem coming our way. I need you to shut the windows that are up here and secure the storm shutters. Then I'll need you to meet me downstairs." Alder's tone was steady, but his pace was quickened. Marla caught on immediately to the severity of the situation, and she moved the pan off of the heat while putting out the fire and covering the food.

"What's up?" Marla questioned while she started on the living space windows.

"Outer Ring punks are raiding this ring on their way to the inner. Looting shops and burning residencies. I don't intend to be counted as either of those things tonight." With that, Alder descended the stairs and set his lift gear to securing the shop belongings into lockboxes that were originally intended to be sold to travelling merchants. Small objects were stacked under the cashier counter, while the larger objects were stored where they were. Alder looked towards the wing mail on the wall and briefly considered wearing it, but he opted to dawn his own fire mail instead. The suit he wore now was originally made for him by his master before him. Like most gear mail there was no helmet, as helmets obstructed the use of gears. The torso was shaped like a metal barrel that was slipped on over the wearer. The entire suit had been made of a single piece of metal that had been hollowed out and engraved with a bird on the chest. The rest of the fire mail was bare. As the suit was worn, the barrel contracted to fit Alder's frame with the excess metal stretching outwards and downwards to protect the arms and legs of the wearer. The bird in the center began to glow with a red light, and Alder felt the heat from the suit washing over his body, lighting up his eyes in the same manner as the bird. He was now in sync with his gear mail and felt the intensity of the steel willing him to watch the world burn. Alder steadied his breathing to prevent the suit from pushing him to arson and prepared for the invasion.

As the first fires began to ignite in the distance, Alder stood ready in front of his own door. He would not lose his life. He would not lose his home. He would not lose his shop. Most importantly, he would not lose his legacy.

RAID ON EBB

The first group arrived at Alder's shop and broke the door down, but they had come unprepared for what was inside. Alder stood in the center of his shop and produced a searing orb of heat from the fire mail. The transparent orb struck a young man amongst the five would be pirates and broke the will of the other four. The young urchin from the Outer Ring could not even produce a scream from the intense pain he felt as the heat ignited his clothing instantaneously and seared his face and neck. Alder felt the pain of regret for the boy's life that he had taken, but it was not the first raider he had been forced to kill, and this night showed him it would not be the last. The four raiders that surrendered were allowed into the corner of the shop, and Marla arrived down the stairs in time to bind the hands and legs of the captives. She had changed aprons and was now wearing a metal apron that served as a fire gear. During her training and apprenticeship she had used this apron exclusively for shaping gears and protection from the extreme heat, today she would be using this to prevent Alder from incinerating her with his assaults. When she had finished binding the bodies of the four captives, Marla spotted the dead raider just outside the doorway. A look of shock crossed her face from the sight of the seared flesh.

"Is he..." She started slowly.

"Yes. He is dead. I hit him square in the jaw with that last shot. If you can't handle to see the dead, then I'll need you to go upstairs and wait this out. I've fought off raiders several times, and every time they try to prey upon those that can't or won't kill. They are animals and must be put down like rabid dogs." There was no hesitation in Alder's voice, and the slight ring from the fire mail gave the impression of pleasure in the words he used. Marla could not deny that Alder seemed to be enjoying himself.

"No, I'll stay and help. We just have to kill..." Her voice broke at the word, and she paused briefly to rephrase her statement. "We have to take down the ones that won't surrender and bind the ones that will, right?" Though unsettled at the thought of killing a living human, Marla used her lift gear to float a pack of twenty marbles around her body. She began to orbit herself with the marbles to pick up velocity. *Not too fast*

. She chided herself to keep the speed down. She intended to knock out her opponents instead of killing them.

"Better get them a little faster, otherwise it won't even be enough to knock down an enemy." Alder had responded to her tactic without looking back. He knew the girl would never kill a man. He also knew that she was going to put the both of them in danger because of her resolve not to kill, but that was just another part of his apprentice that the old smith had come to adore. She had always been compassionate and had built a sense of goodwill towards the world that made Alder ashamed of his own good fortune. He enjoyed his life the entire time he had lived it, but there were a few moments when he had regretted not being more charitable towards the less fortunate. Marla had shown up to his home several times during her youth without having eaten first. When Alder pressed her for an explanation, he found she had given up her food that morning to one of the poorer members of the community. She had a heart of gold, and it was going to be a hindrance tonight. "Looks like another group is coming, must've heard the commotion."

A new group of five rebels arrived at the doorstep to the shop. This group paused before stepping into the doorframe, feeling the intense change in temperature. The brisk night air outside had taken the traits of a hot dessert day while in front of Alder's store. Though they had come from a ring that did not deal with gears much, this group was aware of the suits worn by the smiths to smelt and shape the metal. If it could melt metal, it could melt people, and the five rebels began to surround the shop and break windows. Alder heard the windows break and would respond with a heat orb through the broken window, but he could not manage to track or hit the rebels that were enticing him. The windows were just too small and spread out for him to get a definitive target to attack.

"We need to move towards the corner of the shop. I can't keep track of all the attackers from in the front." Alder spoke quietly to Marla, as he began to slowly work his way to the corner. Marla paused for a moment before halting Alder's movements with a hand gesture.

"I can see them with my lift gear. There are five of them, and one is climbing up the side of the building towards the upstairs windows." Marla gestured towards the back of the building as she spoke, pointing towards the intruder.

"I can't very well hit him through the building, but we can surprise him when he trots down the stairs. Until then, let's see if we can cook the rats crawling around the building. Let me know when one of them is under a window." Alder smiled a bit as he prepared another orb, but this one was not transparent. The fire at the center was easily visible to a casual onlooker as the oxygen in the air was combusting between his hands. The four captives in the corner let out a pained sigh from the heat, prompting Marla to position herself between Alder and them to block the heat. Sweat began to bead on Alder's brow despite the fire gear in the suit. Marla pointed towards a window.

"There!" She let out a yell, and the orb was released. The ball of fire shot out of the window, but then remained in place just outside of the building. Alder had caught the orb with his lift gear. The wooden window shutter ignited instantaneously from the ball of heat, and a scream came from beyond the building. The screaming continued for a few minutes before finally stopping. "Oh..." A slight gasp at the horror that had occurred was all Marla could manage before the upstairs door opened.

The rebel jumped from the top of the stairs and aimed for Alder with a spear. Alder turned the orb of fire upon the man, but there was no force within the orb capable of pushing the man out of his path, and Alder was struck with the blade of the spear. It was aimed at his neck but lanced his shoulder instead. The pain of the wound was immediately replaced with the searing pain of the heat upon the wound as the burning corpse fell upon him. The three remaining rebels rushed through the open door and charged at Alder. Alder threw the charred body at the attackers and prepared another heat orb, but a slight scream from Marla stopped him from finishing his attack. The four captives have freed themselves of their bonds, and one of them had placed a knife at Marla's throat.

"That'll be enough of this." The woman with the knife called out to Alder. "We only came for the gears. You can make more, but we need them to live a good life. Now power down fire boy." As she spoke, the other three captives removed the fire gear from Marla causing her to wince in pain from the intense heat in the shop. Alder's eyes softened at her pain, and he lowered the heat he had been building. The bird etching began to shift back into a colorless bird upon the suit, as the cold moved back into the shop. Alder powered down but remained silent as the three from the door began to collect gears from the store.

"What about this one?" One of the rebels approached the wing mail hanging on the wall.

"Is it a gear?" The woman asked sarcastically, gaining a nod from the man at the wall. "Then take it." The woman continued to hold Marla hostage during the looting of Alder's shop, all the while keeping her eyes locked on Alder. Alder waited, biding his time, as he tried to think of a way out of this situation. Alder was biding time he did not have, and the next question asked made him quickly aware of what the situation had devolved into.

"What about the one he's wearing?" The rebel that had snatched the wing mail asked wickedly, as he approached Alder.

"Of course we will need that one too, but we won't need the

wearer." As the woman was finishing her sentence, the looters plunged their spears and blades deep into Alder's body. He had made an attempt to turn his suit back on, but he was no soldier or gear mage. He had been born into a smithing family, he had been raised as a smith, he had lived as a smith, and now he died as a smith. His skewered body stood now only due to the multiple spears propping him up. Marla let out a cry and attempted to go to Alder's corpse, but the knife at her neck cut her as she moved, and restrained her from taking any further motions. All she was able to do was sob silently and curse the entire crew that had taken her beloved master from her life. Anger settled into her core.

"That's everything, and we even got us a trophy to take along to keep the men happy. I'm sure they'll love you." The woman gave an impish grin as she pushed Marla towards the men in her crew. Marla's anger shifted to fear as the men's hands came upon her. They searched her thoroughly to check for hidden weapons or gears, all the while they were ripping pieces of Marla's outfit. Marla's eyes widened in panic as her mind played out the situation she had found herself in. Six dirty men from the Outer Ring were holding her down as their hands were wandering over her body. Their eyes betrayed their lust, and a few had their tongues slightly outside of their mouths like dogs salivating over meat. Knives and men were holding her in place, and she was beginning to accept the knife as the lesser evil. Suddenly the moment was interrupted by the woman that was leading the pack of wild animals.

"Not now! This is not the time or the place for this. We have to get to the *Daisy* before the time limit or Captain Flint will leave without us." Though she spoke of the haste that was needed, Marla caught a feeling of sympathy in her tone and almost felt pity from the woman. This woman had not wanted things to escalate to the point of no return, and Marla knew it now. She had only intended to scare Marla into complying quietly. She needed Marla for some unknown reason.

The rebels tied Marla to a pole from one of the spears of the dead, then a couple of the men hoisted her up like a captured hog and marched off through the night. Marla looked around and considered her situation. She was tied to a pole, wearing a damaged shirt, had no gears on her, and was just out of reach of getting her lift gear back. She could still feel the lift gear's presence within her mind. If it were just a little closer to her she might be able to attain it, but the person holding it seemed to be aware of her grasping mind and would lag slightly as she reached. Despair pushed into her mind and tried to take root. Marla wanted nothing more than to embrace the sorrow she felt over her situation, but there was another feeling that swelled up within her strong enough to make her fight this outrageous circumstance. Rage. Marla held onto her unbridled rage at the loss of her master.

As a child, she had been fascinated with the man. He had always been strong yet gentle. She had viewed him with childhood wonder and believed him to be a giant amongst men. As an adult, her belief in him had altered. She still saw him as a giant, but it was no longer his size difference compared to a little girl that had given the impression. She now saw him as a giant amongst his peers due to his mastery of the craft and the respect the merchant lords held for him. As he aged, she had taken to nurturing him. She made sure he had his meals on time and pressed him to see a doctor at even the slightest illness. In a way, Marla had come to love the old man that had taken her into his home, and these murderous rebels had taken her happy lifestyle from her. Alder would never see her complete her own masterpiece, never see her take over the shop, never see her marry, and he would never see her begin training another smith. Her blood boiled within her veins, demanding justice against all of the rebels.

During the trip through the Second Ring, the rebels that carried Marla did not stop at any of the other shops. The marched up a path that seemed at first to be randomly chosen, but Marla soon believed that they were following some sort of map. Her suspicions were confirmed when the gang stopped at the wall to the Inner Ring in front of an oddly shaped symbol. On the otherwise clean wall was a picture of a rat eating its own tail. The picture seemed to have been hastily scrawled onto the wall using a piece of charcoal. The woman walked up to the picture and let out a low call.

"Hello?"

"Good evening. Are you finished eating?" A reply came from the other side of the wall.

"Yes, and we have brought the leftovers with us. We have scraps and two meals. We also have a cook with us." The woman spoke plainly back, spending no time to think about the words she was using. Marla guessed that she was the 'cook' within that code.

"A cook? That is quite the leftover to bring." As the voice replied, a rope ladder was tossed over the wall for the rebels to use. The two men holding Marla set her pole up against the wall while the first one climbed over. The man left behind placed his hand directly on Marla's hip and gave her an evil smile while he balanced her in place. When the first man was up, the second grabbed Marla and pushed her up the wall to the first man, who took the opportunity to grope her along the way. There was no fear left in Marla, or compassion, or pity.

"You are only going to make this worse on yourself." Marla's voice was low with anger. "I will make you regret this."

"Pretty lip service from a prisoner. I would expect no less." The first man responded.

"We'll break that defiant spirit soon enough, don't you worry about that." The second man chimed in.

The pirate band had made it into the Inner Ring with their prisoner still bound, and Marla noted the stillness in the air. This ring was undisturbed by the commotion that was now audible in the Second Ring. From her position on the pole, she could see the contrast in the skyline across the wall. The Second Ring was lit up from the fires that were being spread, while the darkness of the Inner Ring attempted to squelch the light. The sounds of panic roared across the wall, yet the silence in the Inner Ring indicated the uncaring nature of the population. She saw shutters close as the band of pirates passed them and managed to locked eyes with a man no more than five feet from her as she was being carried off. He was a middle aged man with short black hair and a short black beard that merged together. He was trimmed and clean, dressed in fine silks, and holding a mug in his left hand while casually closing the shutters with his right. His dark brown eyes locked onto Marla's green eyes and, for a moment, seemed sympathetic to her trouble, but the man dismissed sympathy and closed the shutter. *Don't let sadness settle in,* Marla told herself as she watched her hope of rescue disappear behind uncaring eyes.

The pirates continued through the Inner Ring is a mostly silent fashion. A few of the men had disturbed a trash can set on the corner of the street, but after a shushed moment of panic the gang continued moving with more confidence. They traveled up an incline walkway that went over a grand bridge overlooking one of the many Inner Ring courtyards. The stone bridge that now stood had been built on top of the existing wooden bridge that was put up during the construction of the sky dock, and the original boards had been incorporated as a path of wooden planks in the middle of the stone walkway. The decision had been made to prevent the cost associated with removing the wooden bridge after construction of the stone bridge had been completed. Marla could not help but consider the wooden planks to be the same as her. They had been trapped in place by uncaring people that did not wish to remove them later, and she was still trapped due to the same uncaring nature of the city. She was surrounded by monsters and beasts, but she could still determine which ones were the worst.

Marla's exodus from the Second Ring to the sky dock had taken a little more than three hours to accomplish, but the leather straps digging into her body from the bonds and the pole made the trip last an eternity within her mind. She had spent several lifetimes tied to this pole waiting for something to happen to give her the chance to challenge her aggressors, but she had instead arrived at the final destination and was confronted with a silent sky dock. The sky ships were settled in quietly for the night, and the lights were off on the outside of the inns. Though she had not been to the sky dock often, Marla had never seen or heard of it being this silent.

"Where is everybody?" Marla spoke the question out loud without thinking.

"The festival is coming up. Everyone sleeps early today. The docks will be empty, just like Captain Flint said." The woman answered back with a tone of awe as though she did not believe her own words. The stalls were empty and locked up. Even the guard shacks were cleared out, but Marla discovered a different reason for that while the gang passed one by. Inside the shack, Marla saw a couple of bodies lying on the floor motionless. The pirates had already made their way up here, and Marla did not require long to guess the state of the guards. The pirate woman had looked in the room as well. Once again, Marla could almost feel the emotion of the woman, but this was not pity for the guards she felt. It was confusion. Marla could almost feel the woman's confusion at the situation she was in, and she felt an understanding for the situation as though she had known this woman for years. With nothing better to do, Marla closed her eyes and concentrated on the feeling she was getting.

She saw herself in the woman's place, and realized this was not a woman as much as a girl. Marla had not bothered to look at her before this moment, but now she saw this person as a thin framed wisp of a girl. From the strange connection that Marla had made, she discovered this girl was fifteen years old. Her small frame was well toned and tanned from years of hard labor in the sun, and it gave her a boyish appearance at first glance. Her brown hair was cut into an uneven bob that fell at her shoulder blades as a tangled mess that was pulled into a ponytail tied up with a small red ribbon, and her dull blue eyes that had lost their shine from years of abuse at the hands of men. She had joined this band of pirates as a means to escape her wretched life. She had been awed by

Captain Flint and held him in a special place in her world. Marla felt it as something close to love but not quite. *Admiration, maybe?* He was an idea to this girl, a promise of a better life. He could have been anything or anyone, and she would have felt the same. Yet, Marla felt hesitation in the girl. This little girl had opened her mind to Marla due to regret for Marla's eventual fate. She had not intended for anyone to hurt as she had. She did not want this. Though the men around her had called her Dig or Digit, Marla found a word from this girl's vocabulary that had been all but lost to her.

"Rebecca." Marla said the name in a reverent whisper, as though she were speaking of a dead person. Digit responded with a brief look of sorrow and shock at hearing the name, but quickly overwrote the look with apathy.

"You say something?" Digit replied back while cocking her head, but Marla did not respond. The moment between them was gone, and Marla's link gradually subsided.

The band of pirates stopped outside of the grand sky ship *Daisy*. She floated gently above the dock, tethered by a single chain to a metal ring on the ground. Her bottom was flat with a forty five degree incline occupying a fourth of the front. The front was opened like a mouth and gave access to the cargo hold that occupied the entirety of the bottom floor. The crew was busy rolling supplies into the cargo hold and lashing them down for the trip, and it was composed of a few women but mostly men. Above the ground floor was another level that occupied the entirety of the ship and led to the deck on the third floor. The captain's quarters was positioned on the back of the deck and resembled the shops in the Second Ring so much, that Marla was certain she knew the layout of the inside. The ship towered over the people loading supplies into it and gave a sense of impending doom.

Marla was brought inside the *Daisy* and stored in the brig with almost thirty other women who were all fit and in their early twenties. From the composition of the crew and prisoners, Marla was beginning to paint the picture of her purpose on the ship.

FLIGHT OF THE DAISY

Matthew stood at the helm of the ship in front of a large set of gauntlets that were tethered to the ship. These gauntlets controlled the ship's flight, docking, doors, and weapons and were called pilot gear. Most of the smaller flight vessels had a control gear that was a single stick that was planted in the vessel itself. Matthew had used those often on skimmers and intercity transport ships while he had worked for a wealthy merchant, but he had never tried his hand at pilot gear. He dared not touch the gear until the crew had loaded onto the ship, for fear that he might skim the ship downward and crush his crew or unload the charge off the mounted lightning gear and draw unwanted attention to his endeavor. So Matthew stood still and contemplated what to tell his crew in the event of a botched escape or shoddy piloting to prevent a mutiny. A smirk crossed his face at the thought. He had not been captain for a day, and he had already heard complaints from the crew and lost track of all the crimes they had committed. Though Matthew had no love for the rules and law of Ebb, he had not intended the volume of bloodshed that had occurred due to wanton destruction from wicked men. He had also not seen the women that had been smuggled on board his ship. While Matthew may have been unaware of the actions of his crew, he was well aware of the military efforts of Ebb and the fact that they were on their way to stop the *Daisy* from sailing off. The pilot gear had a message system that went through the ship, and Matthew was forced to use it. He gently slipped his hands into the oversized gauntlets and waited a moment to feel out the information that was being conveyed from the steel. The shipped demanded to fly.

The *Daisy* was a wild mare that wished only to soar through the clouds, and that wish was being imparted upon Matthew in a vision of clouds rushing past him.

"All aboard that is coming aboard crew! We cast off now!" Matthew barely muttered the words as they echoed through the far chambers of the ship. The high powered lift gear in the sky ship allowed Matthew a clear view of the number of people within and without the ship, though he could not distinguish any of their features. He could almost see the people as blobs of moving mass shuffling equipment into the hold and shutting the exterior entrances.

"Now or never." Matthew whispered to himself and was relieved to not hear the whisper echo through the ship. He flexed his hands slightly and felt the ship gently lift upwards. The military of Ebb had arrived at the *Daisy*'s port. He pulled his hands in a rising fashion, and the ship rose to respond, ready to fly freely. The military was halfway down the port and had prepared grapple hooks to catch the ship. With a motion, Matthew willed the ship to fly for the entryway, and the *Daisy* accepted the command. The sky ship tugged the chain apart that was holding it in a single pull and flew out of the sky dock, narrowly dodging hooks from the military.

Matthew laughed with exhilaration from the feeling of piloting in the dark of night. His vision offered him little use for directing the ship, but the feel of the world around him from the lift gear gave the sensation that Matthew had become the ship herself. With a few motions, he could give a test pull on objects around the ship to see how many and how far away they were. The soft feeling of clouds and a wet feeling of rain indicated the night sky had been filled with storm clouds, as though the world itself had risen to assist Matthew on his mission for freedom. He was free amongst the clouds. He was free from his life in Ebb. He was free to find adventure and live the life he had always wanted. After an hour of flight, Matthew could feel the air clear and knew success was his. His thoughts were interrupted by a confrontation that appeared to be happening on the second floor of the sky ship. It was his job now to deal with these types of issues, and Matthew happily accepted his role of governor and caretaker of his ship and crew, but he did not know what he was going to see. He could not have known.

Marla had been deposited in the brig while still bound to her spear. The other women in the room with her had a similar fashion to her own. Their clothing had been ripped in different places, they were bound using any random object that had been found, and they had various marks on their skin from the rough handling they had received. In the scuffle to capture a ship and round of a crew, Marla noted the lack of direction the crew members seemed to have. There were no posted guards, no patrols, and no levels of authority beyond the captain of the sky ship. They were also lacking in proper equipment and training, and Marla attributed this point to the lack of common sense in dealing with her. With the noise of the sky ship taking flights for cover, Marla caught the blunt tip of the spear binding her against the bars of the prison and pressed hard against the pole. With a bit of grunting and a lot of effort, the spear snapped in half at the stress point caused by the leather straps binding her. Though she had succeeded in freeing herself from the binding, she had not accounted for the sharp end of the spear and just missed impaling her face upon the blade as she fell over. A warm feeling on her cheek indicated she had not completely missed the spear, but she was free and armed with a half spear. *Great. I'm in a sky ship miles off the ground with a half spear and no gears.* Optimism is hard sometimes, but Marla regained some of hers by turning to the other captives.
"I'm free. Scoot over here so I can unbind you as well." Marla spoke in a low tone to the other captives. A couple of the women worked their way over to Marla, but several of them remained in place, staring into nothing and waiting to wake up.
"Hurry! We don't know how much time we have." Marla plead with the other captives as she worked the straps off of the two

women who had joined her, but there was no response.

"Hey, I'm Debra Bennet. What're your names?" The first woman spoke to Marla in a hushed whisper.

"Marla Thatch."

"Elizabeth Warren, but you can call me Beth." The second woman replied.

Marla took a moment to size up the two woman. They both fit a similar profile of being slim but well fed, and they were both brunettes with blue eyes, but their similarities ended there. Debra was a shorter woman with a small frame. Her hair was thin, straight, and long with a slightly ruffled look from the rough handling she had received getting here. Though Marla knew she had been kidnapped, there was no sorrow in her features to indicate that she had seen death on her trip up here. She was wearing a one piece night gown that was pink and ruffled with most of the skirt torn off to just barely reveal her underwear. She was the daughter of a merchant and had likely never seen a day of hard labor, yet she was strong willed and indignant all the same.

Beth was far different. She was taller than most of the men in the ship, and was the most endowed of the women in the brig. She was wearing a set of metal armor that was missing a sleeve and the helmet but was otherwise intact. Her left eye was swollen and bruised from the scuffle she encountered, and there was a small amount of blood stained onto her exposed sleeve. Beth was a guard in the military, and Marla noted her as lucky to have her life still and saw the fire in her eyes marking her determination to keep it.

"Great, now we know each other. How are we getting out of here? The door is still locked." Debra opened the question to the other girls.

"We have a half spear. Maybe we can ambush the next guy that comes in here." Marla offered, showing her spear to the other two.

"No doubt they will be coming soon. Deranged men locked on a sky ship with a room full of bound women. It is only a matter of time before that gets taken advantage of." Beth spoke in a quick fashion, leaving no room for argument or interruptions. While she spoke, Beth took the spear from Marla and positioned herself beside the doorway.

"What do we do then?" Debra asked.

"Act like you are still tied up to prevent any suspicion." Beth replied.

Debra and Marla positioned themselves in a sitting position over the cut straps on the ground. Marla took the other half of the broken spear and held it against her back, ready to use it as a club if needed. In her mind, she was playing the events that were about to occur and was having a difficult time seeing a positive outcome. If a single person came into the room they could catch him with the spear, but Marla had learned earlier in the day that fighting can be a noisy affair. If the man screamed at all during the process then other pirates would come to assist him, and the trio of women would quickly be overrun. This problem was made worse by the thought of multiple people coming into the room at the same time. Maybe the men would come in pairs or small groups. There were a lot of captives in this room as to accommodate more than one attacker. If she only had her lift gear. Marla could feel the gear a few rooms down, but she could not do anything with it being so far away. A sound interrupted her thoughts. Footsteps.

"Here they come." Beth glanced beyond the bars briefly before placing her back flat against the wall. Marla watched a change cross Beth's face. All the fear or hesitation disappeared, and her breathing calmed into a peaceful state. Her eyes narrowed and her muscles flexed then relaxed. She had entered a trance that Marla had seen once before of Alder's face. Beth was ready to kill.

The women could hear rancorous laughter from the halls, as the men approached the cell. They announced their intent loudly to each other, and the voiced allowed a headcount to be made without seeing them. There were six men coming to claim a prize they thought they had won. Six men who viewed these women as nothing more than objects to sate their lust. Six men who would die today for this error. The other women in the cell began to sob or rock slowly back and forth, as though they were trying to wake up from a horrid nightmare. Debra had a length of leather held tightly in her hands behind her back, and a few beads of sweat appeared on her brow. Marla clutched her club in anticipation, and the door swung open.

The men stood at the entrance to the door, but none of them entered right away. Instead, these men were arguing over who amongst them would be keeping watch for the captain. From their conversation, Marla gathered that the women in this room were a secret to the captain of the ship, but that news was not exactly comforting. After a few minutes of arguing, a couple of the men positioned themselves in the hallways facing opposite directions. The other four men entered the room. Marla had expected Beth to immediately stab the first person she saw, but instead she watched Beth silently slip into the hallway while the men approached the first woman in the room, Debra. *She left us!?* Marla could not help but accuse Beth of abandonment, and it was now up to her to save Debra and the other girls, but she only had a stick. She needed her lift gear. With her mind made up, Marla stood up behind the men as they began to grab Debra despite her resistance. The men did not seem to notice that Debra was unbound, or they did not care. Marla gave Debra a hand sign to indicate she would return quickly, and she raced out of the door with her club ready to swing. In the hall, Marla swung her club at the first person she spotted and was grateful that Beth blocked the blow. Beth's bloody half spear caught Marla's club in a quick overhead block, and Beth made a well-trained motion to disarm Marla before realizing who she was. The two guards on watch lay dead on the floor. One had his throat slashed, and the other had been stabbed a few times in the chest. Beth had a new wound on the inside of her left arm, but it looked shallow.

"Where are you going?" Beth whispered quickly.

"To get my lift gear. I thought you abandoned us." Marla replied with a hurt tone.

"I did not. Hurry up and grab what you are grabbing. I am going back inside." Beth ended the conversation by slipping back into the room. Marla was awed and terrified of this woman who had slipped out into the hall and murdered two large men in less than two minutes. *No time for this.* Marla chided herself and sprinted down the hall. She felt the call of her lift gear and rushed towards a storage room. She allowed a smile to cross her face at her incredible luck. No one was in the hall at this time, and the room felt empty. Her fortune ended at a locked door. The gear called just beyond the door, pleading to be released from the room and back with its master. Marla called the gear with her hand and her mind. She placed her open palm on the door and pulled on her link. She felt it move, but it felt heavier than usual. *It is the distance. I've never tried to use it from this distance before.* She tugged again and heard it fall to the floor with a loud clang. Her smile returned, and she pulled harder feeling it drag across the floor.

To her right, Marla spotted some of the crew rounding the corner. *I'm too close to leave it.* She pulled harder. The gear dragged closer. The men approached spotted her. *More.* She felt the gear lift. It was just beyond the locked door. The men realized she was not a crew member. *Come to me!*

She called, the gear hit the wooden door. A few splinters fell into the hallway, but the door held strong. The men drew their weapons and began to rush towards her.

"Come to me!" Marla yelled at the door, at the gear, at the crew, and at her life. She felt a will not her own in her yell, as though she was yelling in place of the gear she pulled. The gear crashed through the door and hovered before Marla. It was a pair of beautifully engraved wings attached to a small torso plate that had opened up, ready to receive its owner. It was the wing mail that had called Marla to the storage room, and Marla had no time to question wearing the mail. The torso plate wrapped around Marla's small frame and shifted to fit her size, the excess metal stretching down her legs into leg guards. The feathers on the wings spread open and then shut tight against the metal frame, as though the suit itself were breathing. Marla felt a rush of adrenaline as the suit attached to her. She felt a connection to the limbs she never knew she always had. The wings felt as though she was born with them, but they also felt malicious. The wings were designed for combat and built for war. From its birth the wing mail wanted to reap the lives of the wicked, and that will was transferring into Marla. She felt the wing mail's need for death, and her smile turned cruel.

The crewmen had stopped their approach when the wing mail revealed itself. They had not bargained on fighting a gear mage. It was unheard of for three random men to fend off a gear mage wearing gear mail, and these crew members were uninterested in making history today. The trio of pirates slowly backed off while Marla was equipping the armor. They had arrived at a crossroad between hallways when she turned her attention towards them. Her malice showed in her face, and her body jerked like a puppet on a string. She was muttering something to herself, and her smile and eyes were twisted into an insane grin. The wing mail had taken over, and she was nothing more than a shell.

"She's not a gear mage." One of the men whispered to the others. A gear mage would have been ready for possession. A gear mage would have been trained first before wearing gear mail. This woman's personality had been consumed by the armor she now wore, and it would be awhile before she returned to her right mind. The monster standing before the men crouched down and pressed its wings against the ground. One of the men turned and fled as the other two prepared their swords. The monster's wings pushed off against the ground and launched the beast in a mighty leap. Her eyes gleamed with a purple light and her extended hand aimed towards the men. Marla let out a primal roar, as her mind focused upon the blades that were held out against her, her lift gear peeling the blades in twine like banana peels. She landed in the space left vacant by the blades, and her eyes met those of her attackers. They saw her smile widely, flashing her teeth as her wings clapped together and sandwiched the two men in a curtain of bladed feathers.

Marla pulled her wings back and shook the gore from the feathers. Her twisted smile had changed to a contented smirk. Her eyes had narrowed and calmed. Rage drove her to kill more of her attackers, and one of them was trying to flee. She could feel his presence. She could sense him and track him. Marla would kill the man, but she wanted a challenge. She stalked him through the hallway of the ship slowly, letting the fear build within him as he attempted to find help. She was going to kill him, but she would kill him with others. She would kill all of them. Only then would her rage subside. Only then would she find peace.

ESCAPE FROM BONDAGE

Beth had slipped silently back into the room with her half spear in hand. She would have switched to a proper weapon, but she didn't have time yet. The struggle inside the room had gotten out of hand, and Beth had to admit the efficiency of the men was as impressive as it was sickening. Three of the four had pinned Debra while the fourth had already prepared himself to mount her. The cheers from the ones holding her down were drowning out her cries for help, and the lash mark across the face of one of the men described what had happened to the leather strap she had previously held. Beth stepped up behind the fourth man and placed the spear tip against the base of his skull. With a quick jerking motion, the man was dead and the other three were fully aware of her presence. One of the men skulked behind Debra and held her in a choke hold while the other two were getting to their feet. There movements had been dulled by lust, and Beth quickly slashed and stabbed the two standing men, leaving only the one holding Debra alive. There was no smile on Beth's face. She did not revel in the death of others. The man produced a dagger and held it to Debra's throat.

"No closer or I'll kill her!" The man shouted. He had never seen death before. He was a farm hand before this. He was caught up in the excitement of his friends, and drug along on this expedition. Now they lay dead on the floor, and a killer was staring him down. He would survive this. He was determined.

"Let her go slowly. It is the only chance you have for surviving this mess you are in." Beth responded calmly, gauging the distance between herself and Debra. She was too far to make a move without alerting the man, and that could result in Debra's death. She didn't see the look of a killer in his eyes and knew he was bluffing, but that would not prevent an accidental death from being startled. She had to buy time for Debra to act, or she would have to convince him to let her go peacefully.

"I let her go and you'll gut me like the others. Now, I'm gonna leave here, and I'm gonna take her with me." The man made a move towards the door but was cut off by Beth moving in front of the passage.

"I'll not allow you to leave here, with or without the girl." Beth held her half spear in a ready position, preparing to strike a mortal blow if necessary. "I would rather leave you bound and waiting for your comrades to free you, but if you insist on your hostage ploy, I'll be forced to disregard that girl's life and cut you down."

"Wait... You can't mean that..." Debra's voice shook as the terror built in her eyes. She had been certain that Beth was working a way to free her, but now she could see that her freedom might end up being freedom from life. Tears began to well up in her eyes, but Debra did not count herself dead yet. Her hands were still unbound, and she slowly tucked her elbows against her side to block the motion of her hands from her captive's sight. She slowly started to move her hands up her torso and played up her sobbing as much as she could.

"You are a cold bitch to just leave your friend like this, or do you not think I'll do it?" The man's eyes had widened from Beth's glare. He was still uncertain of his own ability to kill, but he knew that spear would taste his blood today no matter what he did. He had broken into a cold sweat, and the girl in his arms had begun to squirm. His plan was falling apart, and he took a half second to admit to himself that he had never really thought any of this through. He had not considered what he might do if one of the girls had been freed, and he certainly had not thought to remove the spear from the redhead. This was his fault. All of this was his own fault, and that realization had struck him like a club to the head. The girl in his arms was trying to get her hands under his. She was going to hold his knife back to let the other girl stab him. That was his way out, not death but life. He waited for her to make her move.

Debra's crocodile tears poured down her face like a well-trained actress. She had gotten her hands just above her chest and was staring hard a Beth. She could not act on her own. Beth had to be made aware of her plan for it to work. From Debra's viewpoint, Beth seemed to understand what was about to happen. Her grip had tightened against the half spear in her right hand, and her left hand had balled up into a tight fist. Beth's feet were squared with her shoulders, and her body tightened. She was a crouched panther in her black under armor, and her prey was one struggle away from death. Debra steeled her nerves. It was now or never.

Debra's hands shot up to her captive's like twin vipers, and she pushed her back hard against his chest to shove the knife away from herself, but the man caught her by surprise by shifting his weight. His left hand held the knife away from Debra, while his right hand took a firm grip on her arm. He spun on the spot, pulling Debra with him and let her go in a stumble towards Beth's spear. In that moment, he sprinted towards the door hoping to escape while Beth caught Debra, but his plan failed again. Beth did not catch Debra, instead she used her left fist to backhand Debra out of the way and thrust her spear into the man's side. His sprint and her thrust ensured that his ribs broke at the impact point, and for a moment he felt a sickening pain spread through his body. He could not scream, and he would not survive this blow. His chest heaved against the spear that was lodged deep within him. Searing pain occupied the majority of his mind, with regret filling the rest. The man was never a saint, nor would he have even passed as socially acceptable in his life. He was born to be scum and fulfilled his destiny, but now anger began to rise within him. Adrenaline pumped through his body and numbed his encroaching death. He could not be the end of these women, but he could ensure it happened if he alerted the crew.

The dying man summoned his anger and gripped the handle of Beth's spear with his free hand. He took a false swipe at Beth's arm to free the spear from her grasp and tried again to run from the room. He would free himself from these wretches. He would escape long enough to call out for help. He had regained his confidence, but this was taken from him when Beth kicked his leg out from the back of the knee. As the man's knees hit the ground, he felt two hands grip the sides of his head. He was stunned by her power and speed. Her movements wasted no effort, and her hands gripped firmly in a well-practiced motion. The last thing the man felt was Beth's knee connecting to the back of his skull. With his death, the conflict was over for now.

"You hit me!" Debra broke the solemn silence with her complaint. "Hard!" She added for emphasis while rubbing her face. Beth gave her a quick look of sympathy before responding.

"I am sorry for hurting you, but it was the only way to ensure you would not land on my spear as I thrust it. Can you forgive me?" Beth's response lacked any emotion, but Debra shrugged off the lack of emotion as just Beth's way of being. She was beginning to understand her stoic companion a little better with each action, and this woman had just saved her life and the lives of everyone else present.

"It didn't hurt that bad, so I'll forgive you this time. What is our next move? We are still trapped in a sky ship with a small army of pirates." As Debra raised the question, both of the women were busying themselves with freeing the other women in the room, twenty in total, and collecting any weapons off of the dead pirates. "We will need to sneak to the cargo bay and find a skimmer. Two skimmers would be ideal." Beth was testing the weight of a short sword she had found on a pirate.

"Were there any skimmers in the cargo bay? I don't remember seeing any on the way in, and that is the way they drug us in here." Debra collected a set of ten throwing knives from a dead body before stepping away from the dead pirates. She needed a moment away from death. It was foreign to her and offensive.

"I saw one being taken while we were being brought into the cargo hold. We can check to see if that pirate made it safely on board." Beth attempted to free the spear from dead man, but only managed to break the handle. She gave up on retrieving that blade and took the man's knife instead. Debra's face went into a momentary state of shock, as though she just remembered something important.

"What about Marla?" The two women looked at each other and then towards the scared party they had acquired. Beth shook her head slowly.

"We cannot wait for her. It risks too much. We have to hope that she had the same plan as we have made and meets us in the cargo bay." Though Debra did not agree with abandoning anyone, she understood the situation she was in. Debra and Beth collected their party and began down the hall towards the cargo bay.

Marla stalked the hallways. She was strolling casually down the corridors. The smirk on her face only changed when she encountered another living creature. At those times, her face twisted into a wide toothy grin, and her eyes lit up with delight. Every motion of the wings made her body jerk in an odd fashion. She was a marionette attached to steel strings, and she only felt joy at being controlled to kill. Though the pirates did not have a hope of killing her one on one, a few of her victims had managed to inflict wounds upon her. A sword blow to her left arm caused blood to run down to her hand, but was sealed shortly after the wound appeared. A strong blow to her side caused an attacker to realize the wing mail was an armor as well as a weapon, and the blade struck steel before the wings collapsed upon the attacker.

During Marla's deadly parade, she had cornered a group of pirates as they were gambling in a bedroom. The men rushed her at first, but the first man was crushed against the wall by a side swipe by Marla's right wing, and the rest were thrown backwards by her lift gear. The last thing the men saw was a deranged woman lift her hands to her face and laugh at them. The laughter was horrid to behold, and Marla's eyes stretched wide open, and her bloodied hand smeared wet blood across her face. The men that did escape from her wrath were pursued throughout the corridors, but they had avoided Marla long enough to tell the others what was happening. To warn the others about the demon that had boarded the sky ship.

Matthew was strolling through his ship, heading in the direction of the confrontation. He thought of the connection he had felt, the freedom his life had finally gained. For two years he had worked towards this goal. When he had first learned the *Daisy* was under construction from the kind old man in the Outer Ring trade shop. He had a hard time remembering the details about the man, and he could only recall the volume of information the man had about the sky ship. The old man had told Matthew everything about it from the insides to the outsides, from the location of construction to the time and place of the first launch. It was because of this old man that Matthew was able to take the *Daisy* without being a powerful gear mage. The ship had not aligned with anyone yet, as it had never been flown. He was the owner. He was the master. Matthew was the pirate king of *Daisy*, and she would not answer to any other person without a contest of wills. Matthew smiled at the thought. He was not a gear mage, but he was strong willed. In his giddiness, Matthew almost skipped down the corridors, until he heard the screams.

His crew members began to pile past him, running at full speed away from the direction Matthew was headed. They ran as though death was chasing them, and in their chaos they trampled several of their own. Matthew saw the horror on their faces, as he rushed to save some of the fallen crew from being trampled. He drew his sword and shouted into the crowd.

"Enough!" His voice was echoed by the ship and rang through the corridors. The mob halted as they saw the blade in his hands. It was a gear, etched and engraved with the identifiable water lines running through the steel and the discoloration that made the blade appear to be made of bark.

"Clear the way for me to handle whatever you are fleeing from and retreat if you must, but you will help your crew members to their feet and cease the trampling. We are family now, and family does not trample itself." Matthew spoke as calmly as he could to the crew about him, as he stood over the crew member he had saved. She was a wisp of a girl that was staring in awe.

"I'll stand beside you captain." Digit's voice squeaked from the floor causing several of the men to regain their courage. If this small woman would fight the demon, then who were these men to run away.

"I as well!" One of the men called out. Matthew glanced about the crew that remained in the area.

"Aye, let's not run from the demon!" One man called out. Each member that looked Matthew in the eyes began to brim with courage.

"Let's slay it!" Something about Matthew had inspired courage within the crew.

"We'll win this fight!" Several forgot what they were running or that they ever felt fear. They were caught in Matthew's influence, unable to resist his call to action. It was the original reason they had followed him, the reason they had left everything they knew and loved behind. They saw greatness within him, and even though they knew several of them would die along the way, the men had judged the risk to be worth death if a few were lucky enough to climb to the top of the world alongside this captain. The gear in his hand shone with a low light and reflected that light through Matthew's eyes, giving him an otherworldly appearance. He did not stand as a champion amongst his men with shining eyes but was more of a specter with a dark glow of death due to his natural complexion and the sunken shape of his eye sockets. A pale knight with a rust colored blade.

"Form rank." Matthew called out, and the crew formed a rank behind him while equipping themselves with whatever weaponry they could find. The men were holding knives, pans, rolling pins, a spear or two from the raid, and a few of the men had picked up empty barrels as nothing else was around. There was not a lot to choose from beside the kitchen. Digit stood with no weapons on hand, but she was wearing a lift gear she had taken off one of the prisoners, Marla's lift gear. Though she had never before used a gear, Digit felt as though she had used this gear for many years. She had gained the connection to the gear when Marla had used it to invade her history. Had she been trained as a gear mage, she would have understood that gears react the strongest and work the best for the owner of the gear, but gears are fickle objects that hold no real loyalty to the owner. When Digit had forced Marla out of her mind, she had taken ownership of the lift gear Marla used in a show of force. Now she wielded the gear as a weapon and stood behind Matthew.

Matthew's raiding party marched down the hallway with a laser focus on the path ahead. The screams of victims echoed through the ship, and every so often the party came across the leftover gore of a failed assault on the demon that war wreaking havoc on the *Daisy*

. Matthew was shaken by the sight. He had only seen death once before in his lifetime, when a man had been crushed under a cart carrying a great load of manure to the farms, but that sight and this one were completely different experiences. The death of the old man by the cart had been filled with sorrow and tears, the scenes that confronted Matthew now were taken from horror stories and were met with only despair. Matthew kept his gear alight. He was not entirely certain of the name or effect of his gear, but he knew it could inspire courage, and he needed it now more than ever. After minutes that seemed like hours of travel through the corridors, the party approached the demon in the cargo hold. She was standing eight feet in height by holding herself up with the metal wings, and she was not moving. The demon was standing in front of a port window and seemed lost in a trance.

"Now's our chance to take the beast by surprise." Matthew

whispered to his crew, and they began a slow advance. The beast turned on the spot, and the wide green eyes of the creature stared at the pirates with an expression of boredom causing the men to freeze in place. Marla lowered herself from the window and stood upon her feet with her wings ready for combat, but her gaze remained unfocused. Her mind had seemingly succumbed to the beast, but Marla still persisted within.

She felt distracted as she watched the pirates circle her. There was something she had been looking at beyond the window, something important. She could still feel the goose bumps that had risen on her skin when she spotted this something outside of the window. She still had the residual fear for her own life and a faint fear for the lives of other people, people she could only vaguely remember. These pirates were not important to her, but her mind was. She could feel the growing urge to lose herself in the moment and awaken in some other part of the ship, away from these monsters, but her softer side had grown weary of the blood that stained her hands and clothing. Her unfocused eyes locked onto the man that was directing the others. Marla locked eyes with Matthew, causing him to falter briefly and look away. Her eyes were full of hate and pain, and Matthew could not bear to look too long. Her pain resonated within him, and Matthew knew that he was indirectly the cause of her pain. He had always known that some people would be hurt in his bid to freedom, but he had not expected to confront any of them. They were supposed to remain faceless mobs of people he would never see, but now he was forced to see the pain he caused. Marla opened her mouth to speak, and a loud explosion rung out across the ship throwing the crew and Marla to the floor. Marla's eyes focused, and she lifted herself from the floor back to the window. The crew had forgotten the demon and looked instead for the source of greater danger.

From the windows of the ship, the warship *Havoc* was clearly visible and was raining destruction with powerful lightning cannons. The *Havoc* had not followed the *Daisy* from Ebb, but had managed to arrive at the location the ship was heading too. From the way the *Havoc* was positioned, it had obviously been waiting. Now the *Havoc* turned its attention and side cannons towards the much smaller enemy ship and attacked the vessel with the intention of complete destruction. Lighting flew from the cannons, and each shot struck with an eerie silence that was followed by the snap of thunder and splintering wood. With the pilot distracted, the *Daisy* sat steady in the air, unable to escape the barrage. The weapons were pelted first, and then the heavy lift gears were peppered into complete destruction, causing the *Daisy* to capsize in the air and fall backside first towards the badlands below. The *Daisy* crashed one mile north of the Ebb-Nenva border, within Nenva territory.

THE HAVOC ATTACKS

Within the cargo hold of the *Daisy*, Beth felt the first tremor from the *Havoc*'s assault while leading the terrified women towards a skimmer. As the ship plummeted, the women had taken two of the skimmer and placed them with one over the top of the other, giving a small space inside for the women to huddle in for safety from the falling debris and cargo. With the *Daisy* finally still, Beth held the others from starting the skimmer. It was quiet, but the trouble was not over yet.

"Not yet. Something shot us out of the sky, and we don't want that something to shoot us again. One direct hit from a full sized cannon would not just destroy these skimmer, but it would evaporate anyone unlucky enough to be on board." The women fell silent with Beth's explanation, the thought of instantaneous death at the front of their minds. Debra spotted the look of hopelessness crawling across their faces and spoke up to interrupt their thoughts.

"Now, now, everything is going to be alright. We've made it free from the prison..."

"Brig." Beth corrected.

"We haven't been spotted by any of the pirates..."

"Yet." Beth added.

"And we were not the ones being shot at, the pirates were." Debra finished, casting a slight glare at Beth. Beth took the hint and attempted to give a reassuring gesture to the women, but it came out as a halfhearted shrug and a forced smile. Debra was not amused.

"We are going to look outside the skimmers and check for a way out. Stay huddled down and don't make any noises." Debra spoke to the women, but her eyes were locked on Beth. Beth took the hint and slipped out of the boats and into the wrecked cargo hold. A few seconds later, and Debra had joined her outside. The two took a quick look at the wreckage to assess the original escape plan. The top skimmer seemed to still be in working order, but the bottom one was destroyed. A large pipe from the plumbing system had impaled the rear of the skimmer, locking the machine to the floor. The cargo had collapsed in multiple locations during the crash, but the majority of it remained intact due to the *Daisy* landing on her back. Beth looked towards the cargo entrance and saw dirt, confirming that the skimmers would not be able to exit from the cargo entrance. Climbing the cavernous cargo hold seemed to be possible due to the cargo that was strapped to the walls and floors still being mostly held in place. With enough effort, a person could climb the cargo as platforms to escape towards the front of the ship. The brief glimpses of lights in the distance indicated the front part of the ship had broken off at some point, and it was likely there was a large hole the women would be able to escape from. Getting the skimmer out would be another task, as the cargo was packed to closely together, and the wreckage had warped the walls enough to prevent the skimmer from simply flying out the top. After the inspection, Beth turned towards Debra.

"What did you want to say to me?" She asked Debra plainly.

"Don't tell those women anymore things about how they might die. They are scared enough, I'm scared enough. We don't need anything pushing us to a breakdown." Debra scolded Beth, but her tone was filled with pleading instead of anger.

"We should be scared. Fear is a good thing. It keeps us alive, and it might help all of us to survive this. This ship we are on is the *Daisy*. It is a flagship class warship designed to carry a general across a battlefield rapidly. The volume of lightning cannons that struck this ship during that last attack gives the impression that we were attacked by either a small fleet of flagships or a destroyer class. It is unlikely that a fleet of flagships chased this far only to destroy the *Daisy*, so it must be a destroyer out there. That means we ran into it, and it shot us. I cannot think of any good reason a destroyer in the EAF would open fire on a flagship bearing the EAF logo, but I do not think it bodes well for us. Fear tells me that everyone outside of these skimmers are trying to kill me." Beth gave her analysis in a measured tone.

"Okay, but there is no need to give that impression to the others. They are not going to handle that information well, and we need them to focus on escaping and getting home. Let the two of us worry about who is and is not trying to kill us and let them worry about living long enough to sleep in their own beds tonight." Debra continued her plea.

"It will probably not be tonight." Beth's response seemed almost automated, causing her to follow up her statement with a "fine" and a shrug. Beth gave a slight smile to Debra. To her, she was little more than a noisy brat from a merchant or a landowner, but she already had the feeling that this brat would win any argument she got into. A useful talent in a different situation, but for now she was a liability. Yet, even Beth admitted to herself that she enjoyed Debra's optimism. It was pleasant to think that this situation would be over soon without any more incidents. Debra softened her pleading to a smile and changed the subject.

"So, how do we get out of here? It kind of looks like we could get out from above, but I doubt we would get the skimmer out that way." Debra pointed at some of the wreckage as she spoke for emphasis.

"Yeah. It is far too narrow for the skimmer." Beth responded while surveying the cargo bay again.

"We may as well climb to the top and look for a solution when we get there."

"Not everyone can climb that wreckage, and several of the women are in no condition to be climbing anything. They made it here only because the way was open, but I am sure they would slip on the way up." Beth replied in her normal cold tone.

"Then the two of us go up and come back down with a solution. Maybe we can find a hole from one of the cannon shots that the skimmer can fit through." Debra kept her optimism turned on to full. Beth gave her a quick look, and her smile returned. That was a possibility she had not thought of. The cannons would have been strong enough to burst the siding, and the collapsed parts of the ship were proof that structural damage had occurred.

"That could work, but we had better do a decent job of hiding the skimmers and the other women first. It would also do us well to find one of the crates with food in it and bring some of that back." Having agreed on their plan of action, the two women brought some packaged fruits and dried meats back to the women in the skimmer, ate a quick meal, and began to climb through the wreckage.

Marla awoke outside of the shipwreck. She was laying on a piece of the ship that had been frayed off in the crash that had been used briefly as a toboggan down the side of the *Daisy* during the crash. If not for a quick push from her wing mail, the little piece of debris might have ended up underneath the rest of the ship. On the wreckage with her was Matthew, Digit, and only a few of the crew members that had started to surround her. Beyond them, Marla saw the wreck of the *Daisy* standing straight up with its back on the ground and the nose a mile further north from the rest of the wreck. Overhead was a large sky ship with a similar shape to the *Daisy*, but it had a set of twin rams attached to the front of it and a far larger quantity of cannons on the sides. It hovered overhead and did not make any move towards the wreckage. Marla's attention snapped back towards the others as the captain began to stir.

"Are you okay, sir?" Digit squeaked while using her new lift gear to move the wreckage off of the survivors. Marla spotted the lift gear and spoke up quickly.

"That is my lift gear." Her voice came out raspy and thick, hurting Marla to talk. She felt disoriented and thirsty. Matthew stood between Digit and Marla and raised his sword in case the demon attacked.

"Did you stow away on my ship hoping to get it back? Did you viciously slaughter my crew over a simple lift gear?" Matthew voice was heated from the loss of his ship and crew. Matthew was infuriated with the idea that a person would do so much damage over something so small.

"I didn't stow away." Marla began, but Matthew cut her off.

"Would you now use your gear mail to cut open this little girl for your device and then casually shake her remains off? I don't know what happened to you during the raid of Ebb, but I know it couldn't have been bad enough to turn yourself into a demon and sneak onto my ship for revenge!" Matthew spoke with passion for his lost crew members and passion for his lost ship. He could have out maneuvered the *Havoc* if he had not been forced to deal with a stow away that went homicidal in his crew quarters. His gear cast a solemn glow on the area, and Marla felt an oppressive weight fall upon her mind, as though the sword was trying to suppress her will. For a brief moment, she almost agreed with Matthew's shouts and felt she deserved the anger he was pouring out at her, but then she remembered why she was in this situation, and her will overpowered the gear acting upon her.

"I didn't stow away!" Marla shouted. "I was kidnapped by your degenerates to be used as a whore after your crew killed my master! You are the demon for releasing your hounds upon the city! You are the demon for letting those beasts carry off so many women... Oh no, Beth and Debra!" Marla's mind remembered who she had forgotten earlier, and she cast her gaze on the wreckage. They might have survived, but Marla could not rationally bring herself to believe that. They had likely died in the wreck, and it was her fault for not saving them. The wing mail could have rescued them. It could have been used to get them out of the ship before the assault, but she had let her anger consume her, and now the damage was done. Tears flowed freely from her face as she looked at the remains of the *Daisy*. Matthew stood confused, but a quick glance at the downcast looks of his crew told him this girl was not lying to him.

"You were kidnapped." He said the words almost to himself. "I didn't intend for that to happen. If what you say is true, then there are others in the ship as well. Others that likely perished in the crash." Matthew cast his gaze at the wreck as well, but then his eyes looked past it towards the nose of the ship. It had landed on its base as though it had docked. It was a silver lining. He pointed towards the nose with glee and called out to the crew that was there.

"Look there! The nose landed safely. That means the forward lift gear might still be operational. We can get on the nose and get out of here before that ship above us sends down troops to finish us off. Demon, I'm sorry about the kidnapping and loss of your master, truly I am, but you need to decide right now what is going to happen here. Either we are going to fight and only one side will leave this field alive, or you are going to set aside your blood lust. If you want, we can take you with us in the nose and drop you off on the outskirts of a nearby city. From there it should be a simple matter for you to get home on your own. I don't want to help you, considering the damage you did to my crew, but I feel it is the least I can do to atone for the crimes my crew committed. I take responsibility for my crew and their decisions. It is my duty as captain." Matthew lowered his sword and gave a quick bow as he finished his speech, causing Marla to adopt a startled expression. She wanted him dead, she could feel it in her bones, but she was no longer certain if those thoughts were hers or her wing mail's. Marla was aware of the situation she was in though. An enemy above with great firepower, and a bad situation before her. She did not feel she needed help to escape, but it would make things easier in the long run.

"Fine, we can call a truce and escape together, but I want to search the wreckage first for the other women." Marla replied.

"Deal, I need to search there for any surviving crew members anyway. We will pull whoever we can from the wreckage and then sail off to safety from the looming threat perched above us." Matthew formed his crew into ranks to the sides of Marla, to give the crew time to act if necessary. Together, they walked through the badlands towards the wreck of the *Daisy*.

High above the wreckage, in the cockpit of the *Havoc*, stood General Nathan Omar staring out the viewing port. His one dark blue eye stared listlessly at the *Daisy* below, as his right eye, a metal orb with a dark blue pupil, wandered around the skies above the wreck. The right side of his head was littered with scars from a previous battle, and the remaining parts of his hair were kept short to mask the spots where it no longer grew. Nathan stood taller than most the men around him at six and a half feet, and his broad build seemed more in line with infantry than fleet general, but here he stood as the general of the northern border. He held a white gloved hand to his clean shaven face as he inspected the wreckage, a quizzical look on his face.

It had fallen too easily. He had only intended to stand the vessel in the air so that he could question the captain, but the *Daisy* had snapped in twine like a tree branch. It was as though the support beams had been sabotaged, which could only have occurred during the construction of the vessel. On a larger sky ship like the *Havoc*, the twin support columns sit open in the middle of the ship, exposed like a nerve, but in a smaller ship like the *Daisy*, the beams should have run through the walls on both sides of the ship. On top of that, the *Havoc* used in line lightning cannons that were designed to disperse the damage over a period of seconds rather than deliver a full force blast. It was an excellent weapon against multiple targets and flammable targets but was not capable of reliably downing a ship. The beams were too strong for these cannons to destroy unless they had already been damaged or were hollowed out during construction. Nathan stared at the wreckage below as his mind wandered to General Richard Sane.

General Sane had been the Commander in Chief of the EAF for the past twenty years. He had fought in the border conflict before that, and his expertise had been sought out by the congress on multiple occasions for public affairs. He was considered a brilliant strategist and a loyal member of the EAF, but there was something about this man that had always put Nathan on edge. The general had always been charismatic and generous, but there were a few quirks that consumed Nathan's opinion of the man and a couple of incidents that had occurred. The first had occurred at Nathan's promotion ceremony for the rank of captain six years ago. General Sane had approached him with an offer to join him and a few other high ranking officers at a bar that night. Nathan's memory of the event failed him now, but he could recall something about the General that made Nathan refuse the invitation. That refusal had banished Nathan to the outskirts of Ebb, but had done nothing to slow his promotions within the military.

The other event had occurred last year, when the *Daisy* was being considered. General Sane had suddenly become paranoid that the enemy would attack from within and fired all the workers from outside of Ebb that were working on the project. The sky ships were never built in one location, but the pieces were forged and crafted in multiple towns and sent to Ebb to be constructed in the port. Only the central beams were made in Ebb on a typical construction, but for last year's ships, General Sane had them all built within the capital. Thus the confusion set in for Nathan. He was certain that General Sane had something to do with the downed ship, but he could not work the angle. If the general had sabotaged the ship, it would only look bad for the general, and if he was unaware of the shoddy workmanship, then it also looked bad for the general.

"Maybe he's just gotten crazy in his advanced age." Nathan muttered out loud.

"Sir?" His first mate turned towards him.

"It's nothing. Deploy a squad to check for survivors. Something strange is happening tonight, and we need to get to the bottom of it before morning." Nathan's crew began to assemble, as Nathan added to his orders, "be prepared to defend yourselves, we are still dealing with pirates."

A small squad of five soldiers loaded into a war skimmer. The skimmer itself was a small boat equipped with a cannon on the front end. Though the cannon itself was incapable of turning independently from the ship, the ship was generally maneuverable enough to hit its targets. The soldiers were each armed with a standard issue combat spear and a set of flak armor to protect against fragmentation explosives. The spear itself had a small lift gear attached to the base to protect against projectiles from the front, and the blade was a small lightning gear to provide a short range attack to the standard soldier.

With the soldiers were two gear mages in mortar mail. The mortar mail looked like heavy plate mail with a pair of twin cannons on the shoulders. The right cannon was a pulse gear designed to fire anything that was put inside of it at long range, and the left cannon was a standard heat gear capable of firing balls of heated air at short range. The lift gear on the chest plate was sturdy enough to protect the gear mage and provide enough lift to carry ammo for the pulse gear. The gear mages took five cannonballs each that hovered in a halo design above their heads. As the team landed, the gear mages loaded a single shot each into the pulse gear and held their ground by the skimmer. The soldiers advanced on the destroyed rear portion of the *Daisy*, spears at the ready for whatever danger might be waiting. The soldiers advanced from the opposite side of Matthew's group.

DISCOVERING FREEDOM

"It's so high up." Debra complained again with emphasis, causing the smile to remain on Beth's face, as she extended her hand to assist Debra. The two had been climbing for over an hour, but the trip was a slow ascent to the top of the broken ship. The women's progress was slowed further by the constant stops to investigate the walls and passages that seemed large enough for the skimmer to get through. They had no luck yet on finding the escape they needed, but there was still another three quarters of the ship to investigate. Despite her complaints, Debra's face was also lit up with a smile. She could feel her optimism brimming within her, and the situation looked positive. They could get out of here. They could get home. Most importantly, they would all be able to get home together.

The women had come across some of the pirate crew during the last hour, but the members that they found were already dead from the crash. The scenes were usually horrible to behold, as the debris had put several cuts and gashes through the men. Debra commented about the odd placement of some of the gashes, but Beth soothed her mind by mentioning the chaos involved in such an event. There were boxes flying around, crates of all kinds, and the floor was littered in discarded weapons or sharp objects that had either been bolted down or held down before the fall. Beth knew something else had killed these men, but she was certain it was on her side. Maybe it had been Marla.

"Look there!" Debra exclaimed suddenly and pointed towards a pile of junked material crates. Beth stared where her friend had pointed, originally unable to see what had caused the excitement. It was just a pile of destroyed boards and some sheet metal for repairing the ship. It had broken its support straps and had fallen against a wall. The straps seemed singed from the lighting cannons, and the sheet metal had a slight shimmer to it from reflected moonlight.

"Reflected moonlight?" Beth spoke the question out loud, causing Debra to clasp her hands together in excitement.

"Yes! Look at the size of that pile, and the singed straps. The cannon shots must have blasted a hole right beyond that junk."

"But how do we move it?" Beth spoke calmly, but she too was beginning to feel the excitement of the moment. *It must be contagious.* Beth chuckled to herself.

"With the skimmers of course. We go back for the skimmers and collect some of the rope we passed on the way here, tie some garbage to the back and pull the cork off of this ship." Debra spoke in her usual cheery tone, and Beth's attention was caught, and her smile held. Debra's plan was simple and involved a good deal of labor and time, but it was certainly the best plan the women had of getting to freedom. Yet, Beth couldn't help but feel as though the whole idea was as simple as walking down the street when Debra spoke about it. Something about this woman made Beth want to be around her. This something made her want to follow her wherever she might go.

"Alright. Let's head back to the others and go home." Beth agreed, and the two women began their descent back towards the skimmers. It was easy going, as the women had already went this route before, but it still involved a good deal of risk. As the women approached the bottom of the ship, they came to a sheer drop that was a ramp on the way up. The floor had collapsed in the time that they were gone. The women scoured the newly made cliff side to find a way down for a few minutes before both the women's eyes stopped at the same location. A rope net that was once strapped to the wall was now hanging by a cord and holding a bag of barrels suspended from the new bottom of the collapsed ship. The slight sway on the indicated the collapsing of the ramp was a recent event, a fact that brought a new feeling of gloom to Beth. Debra seemed oblivious to the implication of imminent collapse, as she pointed towards the hanging barrels.

"Looks like we could jump onto that rope and climb down from there. Then we just scoot up with the skimmers and fly off towards freedom." Debra cheerily noted.

"We need to hurry. Judging from the new damage to the ship, I'd say the support beams gave way during the assault. We only have so much time before the rest of the ship collapses." Beth replied while judging the distance for the jump to the rope. It wasn't a far jump, she calculated only five feet distance, so Beth was certain that both her and Debra would be able to reach it. With the plan set, both women lined themselves up with the hanging barrels, and Debra surprised Beth by jumping first. Beth's heart jumped into her throat as she watched Debra soar through the air, and it only returned when the slight sway of the rope and barrels did not end with a snapping sound. Debra shimmied down the rope with ease, crawled delicately across the roped barrels, and swung herself onto the floor below. Beth noticed a certain amount of skill in her movements that came from practice instead of talent but decided not to ask any questions. After all, it was now her turn to climb down.

Beth gave a quick jump for the rope and managed to catch it with her right hand. Beth trusted the gloves she was wearing and chose to slide down instead of climbing, but she hit the barrels harder than expected, and the rope was weaker than she thought. As her full weight landed on the barrels, the rope gave way sending Beth crashing into a pile of splintering barrels that released a small wave of water and alcohol. The woman let out a small cry in pain as a searing feeling swept through her body, but originated at her left calf. The sudden wave of liquid had knocked Debra down, but she had come out of the mess uninjured, aside from a few scrapes from passing splinters. As she ran to her friends, she found that

Beth had not been as lucky but was alive. During her landing, one of the barrels beneath her had shattered into a small wooden stake that was now protruding from Beth's leg. It did not appear to have completely impaled her leg, but it had done enough damage to prevent her from walking. Beth cast a downtrodden glance at Debra in an apologetic fashion.

"I need something to put on the wound before I remove the object from my leg." Beth kept her calm tone, but her pain was noticeable within her speech.

"This looks bad, but we can still get through this. The skimmer is right over there. We have some extra supplies that we can use to patch you up until we get home. Then we'll have you properly looked at. Come on, lean on me for support, and we'll get you back." Debra crouched down and offered her small frame for support. Though their pace was slowed, the two women continued on their path towards freedom. Despite her pain, Beth's sullen look had changed to a smile while limping alongside Debra. *Maybe this is what true friendship feels like.*

The women returned to the skimmers, but they were not alone with only their thoughts. The loud crash had alerted a straggling band of pirates to the location of the women and the skimmers. A small band of twenty men with a larger man leading the way had crept into the shadows near the hanging barrels. They watched the girls climb down from the barrels and had prepared to catch them, but the leader stopped them from approaching. He could sense a larger prize by waiting, and he was not disappointed when the lone women led him to a pair of skimmers that were filled with the captives from the *Daisy*. The man in charge let a wicked grin cross his face and gave a silent order to surround the skimmers. Tonight, he and his newly formed crew would escape prison and have some young wares to sell. This trip was not going to be a complete waste of time after all.

In the dark of the early morning, Matthew's crew could easily see the search party making its way towards the rear end of the *Daisy*.

The crew had landed fairly close to the edge of the wreck, and the military party had landed a safe distance away to avoid retaliation while descending, so Matthew produced a small pocket watch from his coat pocket and gave his best guess of time.

"Looks like they will be upon us in an hour or two. That means, we only have half of that time to search for survivors before we need to vacate this area and move on." Matthew gave his estimation while staring intently at the side of the ship. The moon was three quarters full in the sky, providing enough light to see the ship, but there was precious little light on this side of the ship to reveal an entrance.

"How do we get inside?" Digit asked quietly. She guessed that Matthew was working on a solution to that question, but she needed reassurance. She needed her captain to ease the feeling of dread that was creeping into herself and the rest of the crew. Her dull blue eyes sought Matthew's in the dark. Matthew turned his head to face Digit and the crew. He had not figured a means of entry yet until his eyes fell on Marla. Specifically, his eyes rested on Marla's wing mail. He raised his hand into a pointing gesture and spoke his plan out loud.

"We will get inside by having our guest tear open a hole in the *Daisy*'s side. I've already seen the damage from the halls and know that she can get us inside." Matthew gave a satisfied smile with his answer.

"I guess it can't hurt the ship any further. I'll do it." Marla readily agreed to the plan, since it was the fastest method for her to reunite with her fellow prisoners anyway. She squared her body against the hull of the ship, and, for a moment, she felt a presence of doubt cross her mind. She doubted the wing mail would be capable of damaging the outside walls of the ship. She doubted her ability to command enough of the wing mail's power to perform her task. She doubted her ability to maintain control of herself afterwards. As the doubt and fear raged in her mind, she thought of Beth and the deep breathing Beth had done. She thought of the trance Beth had induced on herself. Her mind turned to Debra, who had continued to struggle even after being pinned. For all Marla knew, they were still in that struggle. They were still fighting.

Marla set her mind to her task and felt an enormous wave of joy wash over her, as the wings responded like limbs that had always been a part of her anatomy. Marla forced her new limbs against the side of the ship and quickly produced results. Loud thudding sounds echoed across the badlands as the wing mail was brought down repeatedly against the side of the ship. Each blow ripped at the metal in the ship, and the fading moonlight of the night glimmered off of each individual feather. The pirate crew watched on in both awe and horror as the metal beast before them ripped through the ship's hull with malice and glee. Matthew had not yet seen the wing mail in action, and it took every piece of his mind to keep his composure in the face of such a monster. He turned towards the ship above, and a sense of panic induced realization washed over him. He had to confirm his suspicions first.

"I can't help but notice that you tense up before each swing, and you scrunch your face when you command the wings into action. You are not a gear mage, are you?" Matthew tried to sound easy going with his question, he needed to know without offending this woman.

"No. I am a gear smith. I noticed that you have little control over your crew. You are not a pirate, are you?" Marla replied between blows. Matthew smiled at the response.

"No, and I never said I was. I am Captain Matthew Flint, formerly of the *Daisy*, but I think I'll rename her once I get her put back together. I'm a free man and soon to be merchant mercenary." Matthew gave a funny bow as he introduced himself. He needed this woman to be on his team for the current time. Despite all the damage she did, she was still not as dangerous as a gear mage, and the ship looming overhead indicated that a ground search team was likely to be in route to the corpse of his ship. They will have real gear mages with them.

"My name is Marla." The woman in the wing mail interrupted his thoughts with her own introduction. She did not mince words with the bandits. They did not deserve any more information than she had given. They deserved to be buried within this wreckage, lost to the world as nothing more than a painful memory. "Marla Thatcher." Marla was getting carried away by the wing mail, but this time she felt it. She felt the overwhelming urge to swing her wings towards the crew behind her, but she withheld the urge. It was not what she wanted. It was what the wing mail wanted. One final swing, and the hull was open to the crew.

"All in!" Matthew called out. "We don't want to be caught out here when the soldiers get sent down. Let's start our search by hunting down some of the skimmers so we can cart off some supplies." As he finished his statement, lightning struck. A burly man in the back row stiffened and twitched in a wretched fashion before falling over. Five soldiers marched fearlessly towards the pirate crew, their weapons still smoking lightly from the last round of lightning that had struck the man. Their eyes were dim under their helmets, and they marched in complete rhythm. Their weapons all trailed together towards another of the pirates and they fired in unison. Marla, Matthew, and his crew scrambled to get inside the ship to prevent casualties, but several of the pirates died during the escape. Once inside, Marla quickly used the wing mail to push fallen supplies into the newly formed entrance, as lightning sparked through the hole. In relative peace, Matthew took a head count. Three people in his crew survived. Five total if he counted Marla and himself. Digit, Matthew, Marla, his chef Roger, and a bearded pirate name Carl.

"What is going on? Why did they try to kill us without saying anything? They didn't even try to arrest us!" Carl cried out and slumped his wiry frame down against a wall. He sat for a moment and hugged his knees.

"Hey man, get up. We got places to go and things to do." Roger tried to comfort him by patting his greasy hair, but Carl continued to sob through the attempt. The entire ordeal was too much. He had left behind his wife and had lost many friends on this adventure.

"I was just going to be gone for a few months. Get enough money to move into the Second Ring and start a manure business. It wouldn't have been high class, but it would be enough to start a family. I just didn't want to be hungry anymore!" Carl cried out and then stood up. He gripped his knife tightly in his hand and glared at Matthew. "You did this. You did all of this! It was the work of that gear you wield! I wouldn't abandon my life to die out here without you confusing my mind and working it against me!" Carl stood up and pointed his knife towards Matthew, his intent clear.

"Stop! You came here for you, not him. Don't be so selfish as to blame the captain for your own mistakes!" Digit's normally quiet voice flared up in defense of Matthew, briefly catching Carl by surprise, but his surprise ended, and he turned his knife towards the girl yelling at him. His look of anger frightened Digit, and he took a step towards her.

"I see how it is, you're all against me. You're all my enemies!" Carl screamed and rushed for a slash. Matthew reacted first with a swift motion of his blade, slicing Carl's arm off at the elbow with his glowing sword. Carl's scream of anger was replaced with one of pain, causing Matthew to look on with pity and place a second blow across Carl's neck. The keen edge decapitated Carl in an instant and forced Digit to look away from the brutality. Carl's body landed where he stood, with the head just beyond it. Matthew quietly placed the head and arm with the rest of the body, and removed his own coat to place over the severed parts of Carl and as much of his body that the coat could cover.

"Thank you for your service." Matthew whispered to the corpse, just barely audible to the others, before turning to the rest with a slight shimmer in his eyes. "We need to move on. We've already wasted too much time in this spot. The soldiers are bound to find a way in." The crew marched on towards the far end of the upended cargo hold together, searching for the skimmers.

Marla kept her eyes on Matthew.

ESCAPE

"We found a way out of here. Just a few levels up from here is a hole that is buried in debris that is large enough for the skimmers to fit through, so let's rest for a moment and then we will overturn the other skimmer, fire up both of them, and make our way home." Debra revealed her plan to the other girls while Beth was carefully removing the wooden stake from her leg. A couple of the girls moved to assist Beth after watching her wince in pain from the effort, a move that Beth gratefully accepted. The girls that assisted Beth gently wrapped her leg using the torn pieces of their own outfits as the wrapping and a cut piece of the padded seat as a padding to apply pressure. While those two were creating the bandages, a couple others had busied themselves with a spear and an arm from the same chair. They removed the spear tip from the haft and replaced it with the arm from the chair using some wire and strings they had liberated from the nearby braces and boxes to patch their clothes.   The primal looking crutch was no masterpiece and was too long for most people, but it worked for someone as tall as Beth.

With her leg patched, and her ability to move on her own restored, Beth set the girls to getting both skimmers powered up and loaded with enough food to last a six days. She judged the type of ship they were in had traveled for a quarter of a day at least before being downed. The skimmers were fast, but their speed was only one tenth the speed of the *Daisy*, so Beth counted out ten quarters of a day, or two and a half days, to return to Ebb. Furthermore, she was not certain which direction they had travelled which added a few days to the time it would take to find their way home. *Six days should be enough to at least find another town that can guide us home.* As the women looted the crates and barrels, the pirates waited to make their move. They waited for the girls to finish packing food. They waited for the girls to tire themselves out. They waited for easy targets.

After an hour of work, the pirates made their move by striding out of their hiding place. They took a wide walk with weapons drawn, an assorted collection of knives and boards, as they approached the women. A couple of the pirates tapped the walls in order to draw attention to themselves which caused the women to freeze in place as their captors had returned. The women stared at the approaching pirates, as a panic began to wash over them. Their chance of freedom slipped further away from their thoughts with each passing step. All but two were overcome by the panic these men induced. Debra strode forward to confront the pirates, and Beth hobbled behind her.

"Drop your weapons and we will allow you the chance to leave the wastes with us." Debra spoke firmly to the pirates, which brought more than a chuckle to several of the men. The man leading the tattered group stepped forward.

"Missy. I'm not here to barter with merchandise for egress. I'm here to take what is mine and rule the wastes." The man pointed at two of his comrades using his index and ring finger, jerked his thumb towards Debra, and snapped his fingers. "Make an example out of her." The two chosen men smiled broadly and approached their prize, leering heavily at her body. Debra shuffled swiftly and found a small pole that had once been a shelf support. She gripped her makeshift weapon tightly and aimed it at the men.

"Stay back!" She gave her best snarl as she called out and took a stance that she had seen Beth take before. Despite her bravado, her stance was sloppy and her grip was weak, and the men saw little more than a scared animal trying to ward off a predator. She was no warrior, but she was no quitter either.

"I'm going to enjoy this." The taller of the two men dripped lust into his words. The other man, a short fat man, licked his lips from the thoughts running through his own imagination.

"You'll have to wait your turn. I did more to get here, so I'll be going first." The fat man's voice made Debra feel sick. She was sick with the thought of what her failure would bring. She would not fail here. She couldn't. "I can't wait any longer!" The fat man gave a sudden shout and charged Debra, in his hand was a small knife that was made of fractured metal that had been wrapped in cloth to make a handle. Debra swung her pole against the man, and delivered a fair blow to the man's upraised arms, but she had overestimated her strength, and the man did not seem to be bothered by the blow as he barreled into her. He charged her straight into the side of the skimmer and sent a sturdy strike from his fist into her ribs. Debra let out a yell in pain that she failed to stifle. She didn't want this man to know he had hurt her, but she had never been hit that hard before. She dropped the pole, deeming it useless at this range, and began to shove her fists into any part of the man they could reach, but every blow she delivered was reciprocated with a blow to her sides. After the sixth blow to her ribs, Debra's will to fight was draining. The fat man's grin remained as he struck, and he moved his face in to kiss Debra. She turned her head away, and braced herself for what was about to happen while she was pinned and hurting, but the man suddenly let her go. His body went limp, and he fell to the floor. Behind him, Beth stood with her bloody spear blade, which was now revealed to the rest of the pirates, and a look of pain on her face.

"Get into the skimmer and get out of here. You know the way." Beth whispered grimly to Debra before turning on the spot and facing off against the tall man. The tall man looked towards the new pirate leader with a questioning glance.

"She may just be one injured woman, but she killed one of my men. Kill her, and you'll be awarded with first pick amongst those that remain." The leader barked out his orders to the tall man. The tall man turned back to face Beth, a cruel grin across his face.

"Any woman I want. I would have chosen you, girlie, but you've marked yourself for death." The man leered at Beth as he spoke, a piece of broken board in his hand.

"Try me." Beth stood lightly on her injured leg and gripped the haft of her half spear tightly. Beads of sweat formed on her face from the suppressed pain and adrenaline building within her body. It would not be pleasant, but Beth determined that she still had some fight in her. She would have to fight smart. The man took a few steps forward to close the distance between himself and his opponent before swinging his board in a broad horizontal arc in front of himself. He was testing his own range while trying to strike the spear from Beth's hands. Beth took a step towards the man's flailing, winced in pain, and sent a stab towards the man's torso. He reeled back away from the blow. Beth took his retreat as a chance to continue her assault on the man, forcing the man to continue dodging. Two stabs, seven stabs, ten stabs all dodged, each one announced by a slight whimper from Beth at the effort of attacking. The other pirates watching began to laugh and jeer Beth, egging her to continue attacking and wearing herself down. Even the tall man's expression had changed from a man who was concerned about being stabbed to a mocking smile.

"A little bit more and you would have had me on that last one. Better get it right next time, or it will all be over for you, girlie." The man sneered at Beth as he began to flail towards her again. He swung slower this time, conserving his strength for when she countered. He heard the whimper, saw the spear coming for his face, took a step back to dodge, watched the spear seemingly grow longer, and then he screamed as the spear was lodged deep into his right eye. Beth had slowly moved her hand up the haft of the spear, swung enough times for the man to measure the length, and then shifted her hand back down for the final blow. The attack should have killed the man, but Beth's strength was giving way to the effort of moving, and her leg gave out half way through the thrust, forcing her to fall to her knees. Before she could think of her next move, the man let out another primal scream and sent a hefty kick that threw her backwards. He stepped forward and slammed his heel down onto Beth's wounded leg, forcing a scream of pain from her. He began to kick repeatedly at her leg, screaming with rage and pain at each blow.

His blows stopped when one of the skimmers suddenly sprang to life and rammed into him. The pointed nose of the skimmer had hit hard enough to draw some superficial blood, but the bludgeoning of the skimmer had bowled the man over. The pirate crew scattered to dodge the oncoming machine but many were hit and thrown to the ground with injuries in a similar fashion to the tall man. With no time to waste, the women from the skimmer fell upon the pirates, clubbing with oars and boards. The women had been backed into a corner and forced to fight or flee. With nowhere to run, the women fought. They fought harder than the pirates anticipated they could. They fought harder than they thought they could. Their blows were not accurate, and they lacked the brute force to kill their attackers with a single blow, but their blows were filled with ferocity and were seemingly unending.

The tall man was forced to bear witness to the unlocked primal instincts that had lain dormant in these women. His chest hurt from where he had been hit, and his mind worked overtime to save his own life. He got to his feet and proceeded to run towards the other skimmer, towards hope for a tomorrow. Beth saw the look of panic cross his features. His eyes widened in terror, his teeth and jaw clenched, and his muscles tightened as if bracing against the harm that had not yet befallen him. She had seen this look before in shoplifters and petty criminals. In a different life, a different time, she would have let the man flee, but this was not the time or the life to allow mercy. She rolled slightly to her side towards where the fat man had died and took the knife off of his corpse. Beth took a hard roll in the other direction, pain searing from her leg, and sent the knife flying at the man. Despite her pain and position, her aim held true, and the knife lodged into the back of the tall man's throat. He let out a horrible gurgling sound as he drown in his own life. Beth fell back after the fight as exhaustion finally took hold of her. The women came to her aid, put her into a skimmer, and set off towards freedom with a feeling of triumph and sorrow over the weight of what had just happened. They had fought to save their own lives. They fought out of necessity, but they were still responsible for the lives they had taken. There was no joy in the skimmers, not even from Debra.

Matthew's team waded through the destruction that surrounded them. The search for living amongst the rubble was a slow, depressing mission that usually ended in a corpse that had been crushed to death, but occasionally resulted in the mangled corpse of a pirate that had died to Marla's initial outrage. On more than one occasion, the party had to stop and recover from another brutal scene. None of the team had ever seen this level of tragedy in any single location, and now they were digging through it to try and find life. Hope was a hard thing to have in the desecrated innards of a destroyed ship, but a small ray of hope appeared to the team in the form of two skimmers in the distance ascending the wreckage.

"Look!" Matthew called out to the team and began rushing towards the skimmers. He had found life in the desolation. The team raced towards the skimmers, trying to get the attention of the pilots before they ascended past the level the team was on. Matthew took the lead followed immediately by Roger. They had both been raised on heavy workloads, and a short sprint across a sideways wall was not much of an issue for the two men. Behind them was Digit, trailing behind due to a lack of speed instead of a lack of stamina. Marla brought of the rear of the team and was outpaced at the start. She had never been a fast runner or had much endurance, as she spent a good deal of her adult life in a workshop learning the trade. Her lack of breath made her regret the days she spent lazing around after work instead of wandering the shops or joining a sporting team.

Having arrived at the cliff face before the skimmers, Matthew waved his arms above his head and called out to the lead skimmer below. It rose up to the cliff face and paused for a moment while the leader of the skimmer took a look at Matthew's team. The woman glared at Matthew and Roger, the first two she saw, while supporting herself on a crutch. The rest of the women glared as well, their faces smudged with partially wiped off blood splatters that matched the outfits they wore. Matthew stopped waving and stood slightly dumbfounded. It was too much blood to have been theirs, but it was enough to confirm his fear that there had been prisoners on his ship that he was unaware of. Now he saw them, and he knew they had killed some of his men. He knew they might also want him dead. After a tense moment the skimmer carried on, ignoring the party that was on the wall. The second skimmer did not bother to pause. At the bottom of the cliff, Matthew could barely make out the bodies that had been left behind. His or theirs, it no longer mattered. Matthew was ready to leave. As Marla caught up to the others, Matthew turned to address his crew.

"The prisoners have survived and captured two of the skimmers. They don't seem willing to make any sort of communications with us, and I think we should leave that as that. We need to carry on to the cockpit in the other half of the ship and try to rig it to fly us out of this wasteland. That is our only option left to us, and from the silence coming from behind us, I'd say the military has busted through the wall by now. We will go across the wall and exit on the other side." Matthew spoke softly so as not to draw any unneeded attention. The party agreed solemnly, the gravity of the situation bearing down upon them. They travelled delicately across the wall to the other end of the ship. The short trip lead to a dead end, but the entire crew knew what to do by this point. They pulled some thick cargo blankets up and made a makeshift room to dull out sounds, and Marla set to work punching a hole in the side of the wall. It did not take long before the wall was opened, and sunlight poured into the hole. The sun was beginning to rise in the sky, as if to congratulate the party for their hard work and effort.

The warming rays brightened the mood of Matthew's team as they hurried off towards the front half of the *Daisy*

. Once safely inside, Matthew felt the ship turn on at his presence. She still had power and would still be able to fly. The cruiser overhead had not yet left the area, but Matthew felt confident it would leave shortly. After all, there were two skimmers that were about to zip out underneath the cruiser. The best scenario would be a chase, and the worst would be a swift capture of the women. Either way, Matthew knew he would have an opportunity to escape if he shuffled the *Daisy* across the ground before takeoff. Matthew smiled when the skimmers came out of the side of the wreck. He smiled in triumph of fate. He smiled that his distraction was setting off. He smiled because he won.

Up above the wreckage, Nathan watched the skimmers emerge from the ship. He stared for a moment at the ships, before his eyes lit up and opened, as if waking from a dream. His men watched the various devices that scanned below and looked up towards Nathan expectantly. *Yeah, I see them down there. All of them.* His metal eye focused on the small crew that was running between the ships. The eye was a marvel of a gear and gave extended vision across large areas, but the life forms below appeared as dots on a screen to his eye, and it was up to the gear user to determine if it was a person or an animal. Watching them run between the ships, Nathan decided they were not rats abandoning the wreck, but the crew that had escaped into the ruins around an hour ago. Whatever was happening on this morning, it was more exciting than keeping watch over an empty field.

"Sir?" One of the crew spoke up as the rest of the crew watched.

"Catch the skimmers, call back out men, and let the nose go." Nathan spoke softly to his team. "We are going to follow this trail to the end of the road.

"What does that mean sir?" The crew member spoke up again while the others began the calls to get General Omar's orders handled.

"It means that we are being used as a part of someone's plans, and if we follow the front part of that ship we will be able to find out who is pulling our strings." Nathan explained in a friendly manner. Though large and gruff, his crew had come to expect kind words and honest answers from their leader. Many of his crew were here by choice, passing up positions within the City of Ebb in order to work for this great man. Nathan knew this and felt it was his duty to train, educate, and get to know each member of his crew.

In a short time, the skimmers were rescued and Nathan went to meet the occupants in person. No man, woman, or child walked on Nathan's ship without him seeing them first, and one look at these women gave him a volume of information about their role in this fiasco. They were lost, kidnapped women that had fought their way to freedom. Among them, Nathan spotted Debra and Beth directing the other women, and he chose to speak with them directly.

"Good Morning. Sorry to see you in such a rough state. If we had known there were hostages on board we would have went about this whole event a bit differently. I am General Nathan Omar, but, being civilians, you can call me Nathan." Nathan greeted the two cordially.

"Sir, it is a pleasure to make your acquaintance. I am Second Guard Elizabeth Warren." Beth gave a salute as she spoke, but it was made awkward by the makeshift crutch. Nathan returned her salute in proper military fashion.

"Pardon me Second Guard Warren. I should have known based on your armor, but you are missing your ranks and it threw me off. Is the safety of these women your doing?" Nathan's tone shifted to a formal tone while debriefing Beth.

"Only partially sir. It was a combined leadership effort between myself and the civilian Debra Bennet as well as the determination of the women that got all of us through this trial." Beth answered in a tense fashion. She had never spoken with a general before. Debra looked at her friend and noted the pain her posture was causing her.

"Excuse me, Nathan. Um. We've all taken a bit of shock and abuse from last night's events. Is there a medical bay that we can get some of our wounds treated before this interrogation goes any further?" Debra butted her way into the conversation, and her words made Beth's mouth open in surprise. Nathan gave a slight smile in response.

"Pardon me again Second Guard Warren and Miss Bennet. I will ask more questions after you have been properly treated and returned to your families. One last question. Are all of you from Ebb?" Nathan asked the group of women. After a group consensus, Nathan spoke again. "Then that is where we are headed." The *Havoc* fired up its engines and made a line towards Ebb, leaving a small band behind to follow the nose of the ship.

HUNTING

Matthew felt a surge of joy as the *Havoc* roared away towards Ebb. It was finally time to act. Digit, Marla, and Roger had taken seats in the command station, though most of the equipment was no longer attached to working points. Matthew gently put his hands inside the oversized gauntlets that were still waiting where he left them and addressed his makeshift crew.

"Roger! I need you on the bow weapons. Tell me if any are still active. Digit! Operate the scanners and look for any enemy ships. I'll need you to operate both the port and starboard gears, so stay alert." Matthew pointed the oversized fingers of the gauntlets to the stations as he gave the commands, and the individual command gears lit up at his command.

Roger sat in the front most seat and grabbed both lightning cannon gears, two small rings that floated just about the station. His vision was immediately transferred to the front of the ship before splitting and resting on the individual lightning cannons. Being untrained, his eyes moved together to resist the nausea and both cannons focused on the same spot in the middle. If he closed one of his eyes, he could control a single cannon and aim at the side of the ship, but he could not operate both cannons at the same time without aiming directly in front of the ship. He let out a low groan from the strain the gear was putting on his mind but resisted the urge to loosen his grip on the rings.

Digit sat in a desk directly in front of the pilot gear. The desk originally had two chairs, but Digit had moved one to the center of the desk and pushed the other out of the way. On top of the desk were two large scanning gears the resembled overturned plates.

Digit carefully placed her hand on the right plate, and the gear responded by sending information pouring into her mind. She could feel the broken part of the ship and the surrounding area. Her untrained mind was pulled into every location she looked at, causing her to be unable to properly scan the area and forcing her to look at every part of the ship that was visible from the outside. Digit was untrained, but she was lucky, and her tunnel vision settled on the skimmer that was approaching the *Daisy*.

"Captain Flint! There is a skimmer approaching from the right, err, starboard side of the ship. It looks like the people that were shooting at us." Digit squeaked out in a panic.

"Roger, are they in range of the cannons?" Matthew replied. He had not mentioned to the others, but the ship was resisting flight. Though the lift gear had power, it was taking some time to reconfigure to the new size of the ship. Roger closed his left eye and strained his vision as far as he could to the right, but he could not see anything approaching.

"I can't see it. We need to turn." Roger replied.

"Turn. Okay." Matthew said this more to himself than the others, as he willed the ship to move. The bow rocked forward hard, shifting the broken boards towards the front, and then spun hard in a circle before settling with the bow pointed at the broken stern. Roger let go of the rings as the maneuver begun to brace himself in his chair, but Digit had not been as wise and had kept her hand firmly on the scanning gear. The three hundred and sixty degree turn had caused Digit to receive a detailed description of everything surrounding the bow in an instant. The sudden rush of information back lashed in her mind and forced the young girl to vomit onto the desk before falling out. Marla, who had survived unscathed from the commotion by digging her wings into the ground to stabilize herself, rushed to Digit's side to check her for life.

"She's breathing, but I think she'll need medical attention." Marla called out to Matthew. "We should take her to Ebb."

"We can't take her to Ebb, we are pirates. Roger, take out the skimmer." Matthew voiced his complaint and command in the same breath.

"Yes sir." Roger locked his vision onto the skimmer as it was beginning to maneuver away from the line of fire. "Yeah! Fire!" Roger yelled out with excitement, but nothing came out of the cannons, and the skimmer began to circle the *Daisy*.

"I've seen this before. It's gear poisoning. She could die if she isn't treated." Marla continued.

"Roger, what is the hold up?" Matthew answered his more pressing concern as he slowly turned the ship to face the skimmer. Roger locked onto the skimmer again before calling out to Matthew.

"I don't know how to fire this damn thing." Matthew showed his frustration as he worked to keep the nose pointed at the skimmer, which was now highlighted by ten glowing red orbs. The gear mages had used the mortar mail's left cannon to heat up the cannonballs they were holding. Matthew could see them loading the heated orbs as the mortar mail was brought into range. The first shots rang off the sides of the bow, dealing superficial damage as far as Matthew could tell.

"Figure it out quick, or they will board us." Matthew called out with a low tone as the gravity of that outcome settled into Marla and Roger. It would mean a fight for survival if they boarded. A fight against trained soldiers with lightning gears. A fight against trained gear mages.

"We need to escape. We should be much faster than the skimmers." Marla spoke up with her solution. "If we escape now to Ebb, you can probably get a reduced sentence for your crime."

"That is very convincing, and I'll take that into consideration, but in the meantime... Roger! Fire the damn cannons already!" Matthew howled out to Roger as the next pair of heated cannonballs struck dangerously close to the *Daisy*'s cannons, lodging in place.

Roger had a lock again on the skimmers, and desperately tried anything he could think of to get the gear to fire. With both eyes open, Roger saw the skimmer directly in front of the ship. His vision was drawn to the red hot orbs that would not miss a second time. In his frustration, he slammed his fists down, and pulled the rings as well. With a sudden strain on his mind, the cannons fired out, answering his frustration. Matthew saw the attack land, searing the skimmer with two large bolts of lightning that twined around one another as they approached. Roger felt it. He felt as though he had reached out his own hand and crushed the skimmer. He felt a surge of power and potential in the effort. He felt sick and let go of the rings. His head pounded with pain, and his eyes had dried out from keeping them open. He collapsed into his chair to rest, as Matthew let out a victory shout behind him.

"That's the way to do it!" Matthew called out. "Now, let's get this ship to the nearest town, find someone to look at Digit and call it a day."

"She needs to be treated in Ebb. She won't survive otherwise." Marla interrupted Matthew's victory by continuing her previous complaints. Matthew smiled outwardly at Marla and removed the pilot gear from his hands.

"Doctors are doctors wherever you go. I'm sure the doctors in any town have heard of this gear poisoning and will be able to treat it." Matthew replied.

"No they won't. Gear poisoning is very uncommon outside of the city and is treatable in the city due to the gear Mage College being in Ebb. We have to take her to Ebb." Marla's anger began to rise as she spoke and with it, her wings. Now she stood in the command room with her wings splayed out behind her as she argued with Matthew. Matthew's smile had not left, but his hand had trailed to his own gear at his belt.

"I cannot go back to Ebb. I'm sure it is in a chaotic mess trying to find us right now. She would die as we made it in." Matthew prepared to defend himself as he said it. He could feel the anger swelling up within her.

"Her life is at stake here. She believed in you! She idolized you!

You'll just let her die here because of your sloppy piloting!?" Marla shrieked out in anger, a dark look filling her eyes. She did not notice her mouth move into a wide grin. She did not feel her arms go slack at her side. She did not see the fear beginning to form in Matthew's eyes. He had never seen anyone succumb to gear possession before, and he did not intend to break that record today. He held his smile but ceased using his gear. He instead held his arms up and spoke softly to the marionette before him.

"You've convinced me. You are right. We will take her to Ebb and get her treated. It was my fault she got injured, and it is my responsibility to get her help." His words slowly calmed the beast before him, and his mind worked hard for his next step.

With the peace returned, Matthew pointed the bow of the ship towards Ebb and began his trip. He needed a new ship anyway.

Richard Sane was awake at dawn. He had already donned his uniform and had shaven his face. He meticulously checked his short silver hair to ensure that every follicle fell into the right spot. "Every day is the best day of your life." He whispered to himself during his routine, motivating himself to take an extra pass over his own features for defects. His age showed in the wrinkles on his face, but these made him look wise instead of old. His uniform fit snugly on his slender build and hid his belly fat that had been accumulating over the past ten years. His brown eyes were alert and useful, as luck had granted him his vision even into advanced age. Satisfied with himself, Richard grabbed his cane and limped towards his office. His right leg had been injured during the war and recent years were reminding the man of all that he had given up to be where he was. This train of thought normally lasted him the entire trip to his office, but today was a different day. Today he expected news from the front line. A wicked grin crossed Richard's face. "Today the pieces finally fall into place." As the elderly man entered his office, his second in command greeted him.

"Sir. News from the front line has made it here. The assault you expected was discovered at the location you suggested, and the *Havoc* is currently bearing towards Ebb unannounced." Richard's second, an older woman, gave a quick briefing of the news she had gathered from the previous night.

"Excellent, General Nosh. Have you sent communication requests to the *Havoc*?" General Sane responded while sitting in his chair.

"Yes sir, but so far there have been no answer to communications. We have contacted the watch posts to check our signal and have confirmation that our signal is working." General Nosh replied with a grim expression. Any battle ready ship flying towards Ebb had to identify itself before being allowed into the city's airspace. By rejecting communications, the *Havoc* had identified its crew as hostile to the city state. General Nosh knew this rule was absolute and no exception would be made for any sky ship.

"What a shame." Richard said as if speaking to himself. "Nathan was a fine General and a good man. For the *Havoc* to refuse communications. He must either be dead or captured." Richard rose from his chair and gave his orders. "Shoot down the *Havoc* and capture or kill the crew. We will not have pirates or spies entering Ebb. Dismissed!" General Nosh wasted no time and rushed from the room towards the ground to air command station, leaving Richard to return to his seat and continue grinning at the world.

"Everything has fallen into place." Richard spoke to himself, as he locked his office door and produced an odd shaped helmet from his desk. The helmet resembled the flight control helmet from a ship, but it had no connecting pieces and seemed damaged. It hummed slightly when freed from the desk and emitted a faint glow. Richard donned the helmet and prepared himself to complete his plans. A slight shiver ran down his spine, and his body twitched in excitement. He had waited years for this moment.

With steeled nerves, Richard activated the gear and felt his mind whisked away across the city of Ebb, beyond the Outer Ring, far above the farmlands on the outskirts of the city, and into the control room of the *Havoc*. The pilot that was controlling the ship felt a moment of discomfort, before her actions were being controlled directly by Richard. *The ship must stay on course.* He willed the command into her mind, and the pilot gear possessed the young woman. With the gear mages in pursuit of the *Daisy*, the crew had no indication of the possession.

Aboard the *Havoc*, Nathan prepared to call into the control tower of Ebb for the final approach. The communication device was a small orb called a twin gear. Unlike most gears, this device did not have the indentations and grooves that gave away the nature of the item. The *Havoc*'s twin gear had the water pattern gear marks appearing and fading on the surface of the gear, indicating that the other part of this gear was active. Nathan lifted the orb into his hand and sat at his desk. It took him a bit of time to activate the gear, as he had never been useful with anything related to the devices. When fully active, the device was coated with etchings that flowed like water across the surface. Nathan took a breath and began to speak in a steady tone.

"This is General Nathan Omar of the *Havoc* reporting in for a final approach. Estimate one hour to dock. Respond."

"This is Ebb Central Dock, proceed to docking port five for unloading. Medical attention will be on hand as per requested." A soft voice echoed from the stone. Nathan wrote down the communication times in his log, dipped the stone in ink and stamped the log with the pattern displayed, and shut down the communications. He stretched himself in the chair before getting up and heading to the chamber window. Outside was the grassland and farmland over the outskirts of Ebb. A peaceful smile covered Nathan's features. After all these years, he was finally coming home. His peace lasted half an hour, until the walls of ebb came into view, and the cannons began to fire. The use of lightning gears on ships was effective due to the lack of extra weight that would be required for cannons or mortar gear, a defensive wall had no need to care about added weight.

The *Havoc* shook from a direct hit from a large mortar gears. Seconds after the impact, the sound of the shot reached reverberated through the ship. Nathan was already rushing through the ship to the command station when the echoes of the cannon deafened the crew. A few more mortar roars indicated that other shots had been fired with the intent to down the ship. In the command center, the crew sat nervously at their stations, weapon systems fully operational. In any normal situation, the crew would have initiated the counter attack without the approval of the general, but the city was attack, and the crew did not know what to do. To fight back would make them criminals, to not fight back would make them dead. Nathan burst into the command center, calling out orders.

"Navigation, focus your effort on tracking projectiles. Weapons, follow navigation's prompts and shoot them down. Pilot, get us out of here!" The crew set to their new tasks as commanded, except for the pilot.

"Projectiles are now being traced." Navigation called out, the plate shaped gears glowing bright. For the weapon team, they could see the outline of projectiles in the air and made short work of the orbs launched towards the *Havoc*.

"We won't be hit again, Sir!" Weapons called out to the command station.

"Sir, the ship won't turn. It seems we are being pulled into the docks." The pilot called out in a monotone voice. Nathan approached the young woman and saw the look in her eyes. She was awake, but unaware of her actions. He suspected foul play.

"I've never heard of a pilot gear possessing a trained pilot, but it seems that is what has happened, and we are going to the dock. Crew! It appears we have been betrayed and have fallen victim to a trap set by a hidden enemy!" Nathan called out to his command center. "Arrest our guests and a small team of the soldiers. Everyone else, make sure the *Havoc* arrives safely to the dock and prepare to be arrested." The crew looked upon their general with a mixture of fear and respect. They knew that he was already trying to get everyone out of this mess, just as they knew he would need their unquestioning cooperation. In unison, they reassured their general.

"Yes, Sir!"

The ship burst into a frenzy of activity, as the crew quickly dislodged order on the ship. Debra, Beth, and the other women were assaulted in the medical bay by crew members. The chosen crew mates entered the medical bay and fired a couple of warning rounds at the cabinets while yelling at the women to form a line. Debra shouldered Beth, who had been heavily sedated during the treatment of her leg, and limped her along with the others. She wanted to fight back against this new development but prioritizing the lives of her fellow captives required cooperation, if only for a short time. The women were marched to the brig and put into cells that appeared to have been used already but not cleaned out for the next prisoners. Debra's confusion mounted further when two of the soldiers carefully took Beth from her, set her safely in a clean bed in one of the cells, gave their weapons and uniforms to the other soldiers, and locked themselves into cells alongside the women.

Outside the ship, a battle erupted over the sky of Ebb. The city's defenses lobbed shots of metal and lightning, while the *Havoc* rode in with all cannons firing at the projectiles. Scorch marks peppered the hull, as the *Havoc* sailed across a sea of lightning towards the Grand Market. The city closed large gates to keep the *Havoc* from reaching the docks, but the ship's speed increased as the doors closed, and the destroyer class ship rammed through the closing gate, ripping one of the doors off in the process and tearing apart the pulley system that operated the mechanisms. With no easy means of stopping at its current speed, the *Havoc* turned broadside and slammed hard against a wall before listing lazily towards an open port. The city guard prepared for the worst, but the hatch opened and revealed a crew and general that surrendered on the spot.

The hunt of the *Havoc* blinded the city's defense from the front end of the *Daisy* as it parked north of the Outer Ring, allowing the pirates and Marla to sneak silently into the city under the cover of mortar fire. By the time Marla made it into the city, Matthew and Roger had vanished, leaving Digit in Marla's care.

RECONCILIATION

Marla sat alone in the store staring at the door to the workshop. After her return, the city of Ebb notified her that Alder had left the building to her in the event of his death, so it was now her store and workshop. She had repaired the windows and walls and scrubbed the floor and counters, but it still felt dirty. Her life had been here, her happiness, and now it was an empty building that she owned. Two months had passed since her abduction, two months since Alder's death, and two months since the last time Marla had entered the workshop. She survived this time by spending the money she had saved previously for the purchase of her own shop. Though she still had plenty left, staying out of the workshop made the building foreign. On the two month anniversary of Alder's death, Marla summoned her courage and entered the workshop.

The workshop had not changed. Marla could still envision Alder sitting behind his desk. *My desk.* Half complete projects lay around the workshop, customer orders that were understandably delayed, and personal projects that would go unfinished. Marla walked to a bare wall and began hammering nailed into a wall a strategically picked locations. She had mapped out where they would be needed before she went inside and now put her project into motion. In a short amount of time two beautiful metal wings hung upon the wall, close to one another, but not connected in any way. The lift gear portion of the wing mail was the metal spine piece that Marla continued to wear under a cloak. The use of gear mail was forbidden outside of the gear mage corps, but without her standard lift gear, Marla decided to utilize what she already had grown accustomed too. The sound of the bell on the store entrance distracted her from her thoughts.

"The shop is not open right now." Marla called out to whoever had come into the store.

"I'm not here for the shop. I'm here for lunch, and you are running late for it." A friendly voice called out from the entrance, causing a smile to cast over Marla's face. In her shop stood Debra, cleaned up and dressed in a dark green dress with silver trim tracing out a floral pattern. Debra's face was beaming with joy as she looked around the empty shop. "I see everything is finally fixed. Good for you!"

"Why are you in such a good mood?" Marla posed the question while collecting her travel bag, a small brown satchel with a shoulder strap, and heading towards the door. Her questions was answered for her when she saw the group that was collected for the lunch date. There were several of the women that had been captured, all merrily chatting with one another. Digit stood amongst the ranks almost cowering out of any conversations that were struck up with her. Marla had told the others that she had also been captured and was being kept with the captain. In the back of the crowd, standing tall and speaking softly to some of the other women stood Beth, who had finally been released from the medical facility.

"I'm always in a good mood." Debra said in a sing song fashion before running off to pick up a conversation with Beth. Marla's smile held, and she felt that this one was the first genuine smile she had managed since before the *Daisy*. The women traveled to an open courtyard restaurant that was serving a roasted boar and summer vegetable stew. On the walk to the restaurant, Digit walked close to Marla and kept nervous eyes on the crowds around her, specifically the guards. The other women had noticed the increased number of guards patrolling the city as well but passed it off as a reaction to the *Havoc's* silent run into the city. Yet, as understandable as heightened security would be, the number kept increasing week after week. At the restaurant, Beth, Marla, Debra, and Digit occupied their own table and began talking in low tones.

"Have you heard anything about the trials yet?" Debra asked Beth, starting the main topic for the lunch meeting. Beth gave a grim expression.

"General Sane is doing a private hearing tomorrow evening, but I have not heard anything other than that. It does not sound good for General Omar though. I tried to visit him, but the EAF would not mention which prison he is being kept at. It would appear that they are keeping him in a secret prison to keep him from talking to anyone." Beth commented solemnly before eating a bit of the stew before her.

"Have any other pirates been spotted?" Digit squeaked into the conversation, a slight tone of hope in her voice. Since she was dropped off at the medical facility, she had not heard anything from Roger or Matthew.

"No, but there are reports I have heard that mention something skulking around the city at night. The city guard is using it as an excuse to increase ranks, but the increase seems to align closer to the EAF's increased presence within the city itself. There has even been talk of a few fights breaking out between state defense and the armed forces." Beth's comment caught Marla's attention.

"I thought the city guards were a part of the armed forces. Why would the two be fighting?" Marla raised her question.

"You are not wrong. The city guard is the Ebb State Defense unit of the EAF, but it was built to appease the merchants, so all power over the State was given to the Judges. It is not uncommon for the EAF regulars to call us mercenaries, and it is not an entirely inaccurate description. Generally, the training process for the EAF takes a couple of years to complete, unless you are a gear mage. For the city guard, you only have to prove competency in combat and take a short course in non-lethal combat to prove you can arrest civilians when needed. In this case, it would seem someone is driving up the tension between the state and armed forces." Beth explained calmly.

"What about the skulker?" Digit asked quietly.

"I do not believe either side is going to allocate any resources towards the apprehension or investigation of the skulker since nothing has been stolen and no crimes have been committed." Digit stared at Beth quietly after her comment, prompting Debra to speak up.

"She's saying they aren't going to look, because being creepy at night is not a crime." Debra's clarification caused Digit to cast her eyes downward in sorrow. Marla saw a look of loss cross Digit's features, and her heart cried out to help.

"Why don't we search? It would be better than sitting around doing nothing, and it might even give us more information as to what is going on in the city. We can look around the city and ask about the increased tension. We can also find out anything we can about the person sneaking around." Marla posed her question to the group at their table. The women gave a slight pause to consider, and then agreed that it was better to search for information than to sit idly by while the world fell apart around them. "We can use my shop as a base of operations."

As the sun began to set on the city-state of Ebb, Beth, Digit, Debra, and Marla gathered around a table in the ground floor of Marla's shop. On the table lay a large white table cloth that had a series of circles carefully drawn onto the center. The center most circle was labeled GM, and the rest of the cloth had bits and pieces of areas filled in with squares and rectangles and dashed lines. The table cloth appeared to be a rudimentary map of Ebb. Debra let out a low whistle as she approached the map.

"You've been busy, but it looks like you've left out some parts." Debra pointed at an empty space in the Market District to emphasize her point, and the table let out a low glow to trace the areas she pointed at. Debra pulled her hand back in surprise from the sudden whir of the machine, but a smile formed on her face when she spotted the map burning the buildings she knew into the point she traced.

"It's a gear?" Digit questioned meekly.

"Yes, this is a mapping gear. It works similar to the lift gears as far as operation, but this will light up the table with a low heat instead of lifting objects. Alder built this for the EAF, but they never came back to get it." Marla's eyes watered slightly as she added, "that was years ago." The women looked on in silence for a moment, before Beth put her hand on Marla's shoulder.

"Thank you for allowing us the use of this treasure. We can use this to draw a map of Ebb, then we can set areas for us to look around for information about who is skulking around the city, and what is happening to cause tension between the Ebb State Defense and the EAF. Maybe we will get lucky and find the culprit that is spreading chaos or the location of General Omar. I am certain that he knows what is going on." Beth gave the women a call to action, and they began work on the map of Ebb. The workshop began to fill with a soft blue light and a quiet hum as the machine worked. The four women tracing their own images onto the map as they remembered the parts of the city they had observed in their lifetime.

Digit filled a large portion of the Outer Ring, revealing large areas dedicated to people sleeping on the street or the ground. She traced the outlines of several small buildings that held food supplies to the forever hungry citizens of the Outer Ring, and the long roads that acted as lines to enter into such a place. The meeting spots of her former allies were traced in great detail, indicating the length that the fifteen year old had traveled to follow Matthew and spanning a circle around the entire city of Ebb. She paused for a moment before continuing her marking. She filled in the farm houses that accepted extra day labor during the harvest and planting, and she indicated the lumberjacks that would accept helpers during the winter time. Digit filled out a bleak outlook on life built from living in the Outer Ring and finished with the brothels that accepted labor from women of any age. She worked without tearing up or feeling sorrow and labored away a picture of her past that she no longer had any feelings for at all. All that Digit saw was the future, a future that Matthew promised her, a future she could almost reach if she just worked a little harder. The other three women had stopped their own work to stare in amazement and pity at this young girl. For all that she had been through to this point, she was still full of hope.

Debra filled out her section next and brought most of the information the women needed about the Inner Ring and the Grand Market. She showed the different schools that are located in the Inner Ring that are dedicated to teaching the next generation of merchants how to handle the world they will own. She drafted the building where the merchant lords meet to discuss the trades and tariffs from other nations. Debra filled in the many different dance halls and playhouses that occupied the time of the elites, and filled in the small booths that allow for philosophical discussion to take place freely and anonymously. These were small buildings that had curtained off rooms designed to distort the voice of the speaker so that the conversations could be spontaneous and promote new legislation or ideological directions for the city. Debra showed the many different restaurants that she had gone to throughout her life, as her father had tried to show her as many different things as he could. Debra painted a life of luxury and complacency that ended with surprise, as her own house had already been drawn onto the map from the work that Marla had done. Marla and Debra shared a small moment of wonder as they stared at each other, both knowing that the only time Marla would have seen her house would have been during the night of the abductions.

With large portions of all three rings filled in, Beth set to work drawing the walls of the city. Though the city was generally broken down into the three rings, the walls were not built into circles around the Districts. There were several locations on the map between the Rings where the walls encroached more on one or the other. In the case of the wall between the Second Ring and the Outer Ring, the Outer Ring was always losing space to the Second Ring, but the women noticed this pattern did not hold true between the Inner Ring and Second Ring. Specifically, the women spotted a location where the walls seemed to outline something that occupied a large area between the rings. There was a walled off section of the city on the far side of the main road that connected the most successful businesses to the Grand Market. The women knew nothing about the inside of it, as it seemed to occur naturally between the walls.

"Maybe it's a prison?" Debra chimed in.

"No, the prison is located here." Beth marked a small, gated compound on the map and put some buildings within the walls she drew. "I served as a prison guard for a short time."

"Maybe it is a secret prison." Digit spoke up, a sense of childish wonder building within her.

"Whatever it is, I think we should investigate. It looks like a compound of some sort, so it might have information on the skulker, the tension, or General Omar." Debra decided as she looked to the rest. Marla looked at the map, and then to the rest of the women. The compound was obviously being protected and hidden. Marla could feel the danger of this mission. She could sense the reality of being captured and disappearing from the world forever, but she also felt the world around her falling apart from some hidden force. Her will to proceed was shaken by the scale of what the women would be getting themselves into.

"I know I was the one that suggested looking for the skulker, but should we really be getting involved in all of this?" Marla questioned the others while pointing at the hidden compound. "We had agreed to look around the city for information about someone sneaking around, not investigating hidden buildings."

"I have to work for the good of the city, or there won't be a city left to work for." Debra responded with resolve, flashing Marla her soft smile that had won the hearts and minds of her friends. Despite the kidnapping and death that had occurred around her, Debra had remained the kind soul that had brought sunshine to a group of imprisoned women in the middle of the night.

"I am sworn to protect this city, even if I must protect it from itself." Beth's resolve shone with a different light then Debra's, and

Marla knew that Beth would have ended up on this path on her own eventually. Strong and caring, but cold and deadly when needed, Marla saw Beth as a silent guardian of everything the woman set her eyes upon. Marla worried that Beth's resolve would get her killed someday.

"I don't have a past or a future if this city falls apart before I find what I'm looking for." Digit responded meekly, and Marla's heart hurt for this child. She was still young, but had seen so much of the world. Marla saw Digit as a child that desperately wanted to run away from this world.

Marla looked at her friends with awe and realized that is what they were to her. These women had become her friends through bonds forged in chaotic fires. She had failed Alder with her shaken resolve to do what is necessary, and she would not fail again. "I want to look out for my friends, no matter what stupid scheme we cook up. Fine, I'm in too."

With Marla's commitment to the investigation of the unknown area, the group began to plan.

On the outskirts of the city, in the Outer Ring, Matthew had fallen back in step with his old life. He worked in the morning on various farms to get a small wage, stole food from his employers to supplement his living expenses, stalked some of the guards at the gates to hear the gossip of the town, an occasionally would sneak into the Inner Ring to investigate the Market District. The day of the women's meeting, Matthew had found himself deep in the Grand Market, standing once again on the docks. He was dressed in several layers of brightly colored clothing and pushing a cart filled with bolts of cloth in different colors and patterns. Roger was dressed in an equally ridiculous fashion, as he called out to random people. After a few hours, Matthew slipped the brightly colored clothing off and changed into a more modest apparel. With Roger making bold claims about the color of the bolts adding everything from better relationships to longer life, Matthew was able to disappear from the stall without anyone taking notice of him. He had come here on a mission, just as he had done before.

Matthew fell in step with the crowds heading towards the docking area of the Grand Market. He traveled upwards through sloped walkways that had been carved in and around the large pillar before ending up at the loading and unloading station of the docks. The dock workers scurried along carrying crates and supplies off and on the different ships, while the hired hands for each ship carefully watching over the cargo and carriers for thieves looking for a quick score. Matthew's goal was much further back in the docks, so he ducked around the workers, deftly dodging crates. He avoided confronting any of the watchers, spotting eyes and skulking through the crowd to avoid gazes. He merrily made his way towards and empty dock that lay between the merchant section and the military section, and he noted that this would be the second time he had stolen his way into the military docks, and his third time being there. The second time being here had been the night of the raid that had scored him the *Daisy*. Matthew hung himself over the side of the dock and began to climb horizontally towards the military section while reminiscing about his first visit.

The last time Matthew had hung perilously onto the side of the Grand Market, he had done so at night. That night so long ago, Matthew had thought of the women he had known to keep his mind off of the terror of his situation. He had crawled sideways for a half mile before pulling himself into the docks. The new moon had caused the world to fill with distorted images crafted from the shadows and the imagination, so Matthew had ducked and hidden from things that both did and did not exist. Footsteps overhead caused Matthew to cease his memory and climb down a little lower to avoid detection. *This was much easier at night.* He held the wall and his breath as he was forced to remain still. After a few minutes of waiting, the guard above him struck up a conversation with someone else, and Matthew took the noise as an opportunity to continue his mission. He now focused on the noise around him, listening for the guards walking and trying not to think about his tired arms and legs. At the end of the track, Matthew took a moment to rest on a large metal ring that had been attached to the wall. Several of these rings littered the docks on the military district, due to the different sizes of ships that were used.

From what Matthew had learned, the smaller ships that merchants used are freighters and are mostly composed of cargo space. These ships are designed to land when docked, and have proper landing pegs that hold the ship upright while not in use. There are larger merchant ships, but Matthew did not know the names or features of those ships, as he had never considered those as a target for his theft. *I will learned them eventually.* He always told himself, but had not done so. On the military side of sky ships, there are the smallest and fastest ships called interceptors. These ships are designed to hover when docked and are loaded from the bottom for quick loading and unloading. Most of the weaponry on these ships are front mounted, and they are commonly used as flagships for the military. The *Daisy* was an interceptor class ship. *Now she is an interceptor class command deck.* Matthew mused to himself. His current target was a destroyer class ship that had been recently been deposited without a commander, the *Havoc*. Destroyers are side loading ships intended for longer missions. The weaponry is also placed on the sides of destroyers to take advantage of the longer length of the ships. From Matthew's resting place, he could see the *Havoc* floating gently on the docks nearby.

Matthew took his rest to wonder if the ring he was now sitting on was the same ring he had rested on the last time he was here. He had rested quite a deal longer the last time, as he had not known the exertion that this expedition was going to place on his body and had rushed his climb. The last time he was here, Matthew had climbed up at the ring he rested on and was immediately accosted by a man watching the docks. Matthew smiled at his own naivety while remembering the scene. There he was, a young man with nothing but a trench coat and an iron will sneaking into a militarily controlled district trying to talk his way out of a situation he was certain would not have happened. He was chasing a cat was the best excuse he could think of at the time, so he had decided to stay silent instead while the man looked him over. Surprisingly for Matthew, the man did not arrest him or have him arrested. Instead they man gave him the sword that he is now carrying, told him about the *Daisy* and sent him on his way. Even now, Matthew knew the man was trying to use him for his own gain, but if it meant gaining a ship and freedom from the Outer Ring, Matthew was willing to be used.

Sufficiently rested, Matthew continued his climb over to the dock that the *Havoc* was tethered to. He gripped the chain that held it in place and climbed his way onboard the ship through one of the canon ports. From his coat pocket, Matthew pulled out a small notebook and a pen. He strolled through the empty halls of the *Havoc*, taking notes on the size and facilities that were on board, before heading back to the canon port he had entered from. The entire trip had taken him a couple of hours, but he had been unhindered by anyone coming into or leaving the ship. He could not help but smile broadly as he shimmied back down the chain at the ease of his mission. As he transferred his body from the chain to the ring, a voice greeted him from above.

"Don't move." The voice calmly ordered before continuing, "We've been expecting you."

"Expecting me?" Matthew asked while trying to figure out how many guards were above him. *At least one. The shuffling of feet sounds like more though. Could be a squad.* His eyes roamed around him for an exit, but the only way out was down. He was not that crazy.

"Of course. Who climbs into a destroyer class ship that is being locked out for an investigation in the middle of the day? We watched you go in, and were given the orders to apprehend you when you come out. It would seem today is an unlucky day for you, as General Sane has requested you get taken straight to him."

The guard explained.

"What about my trial and hearing? I shouldn't be going straight to the High General over trespassing." Matthew was reconsidering the jump.

"No such luck, I'm afraid." The guards put small poles with blunt metal hooks down by Matthew. "Grab a hold and allow yourself to be peacefully taken to the general. We don't want any accidents today." The guard spoke without any malice, so Matthew grabbed the poles and allowed himself to be arrested, mentally kicking himself for being so naive a second time.

GENERAL NATHAN OMAR

General Omar stood proudly as a beacon of dignity. His hands were tied above his head and bruises covered his exposed chest. His lip was bloodied from rough handling, and his left eye had been swollen shut. Despite the beating he was taking, he still smiled at the dungeon master when he entered the dark room. Nathan did not blame this man for doing his job. The dungeon master entered the room with a bucket of hot coals in one hand and an iron rod in the other. His expression was a mixture of grim determination and solemn pity. Neither party wanted to be in the room for this event. The dungeon master began this day as he had the previous ones, hoping today would be the last day he would have to interrogate this general that stood before him.

"State your name." The dungeon master called out.

"General Nathan Omar."

"State your assignment."

"I am the acting sky ship general of the Ebb-Nenva Border and captain of the *Havoc*."

"Why was the *Havoc* in the capital on the 3rd night of the second lunar cycle?"

"I was returning a group of civilians that had been kidnapped from Ebb."

"Why did you not call for a transport?"

"I called for a transport but received no answer."

"Why is there no evidence of these calls being made in the Ebb communication logs?"

"The evidence exists on my communication log in the *Havoc*."

"The communication log that is not there?" The dungeon master raised his voice on this question. He had asked it before. He had asked it every day since the soft spoken general had been put in his care, and he had received the same answer he knew was coming.

"The communication log that is not there." The general responded. The dungeon master stared at this man in wonder before asking the next question. He asked because he had to. It was his job to ask, and his job to respond to the answer he knew he would get.

"Where is the communication log?" The dungeon master asked with a sigh.

"I do not know the location of the communication log from the *Havoc*." General Omar responded while staring intently at the dungeon master. The dungeon master stared back for a moment, before turning his attention to the bucket of hot coals with the iron rod inside. The rod had turned half red from the heat, and the dungeon master grabbed it safely by the handle. He turned back towards the general with an apologetic look on his face.

"Let's begin the interrogation then." The dungeon master started. "State your name!" This time the man yelled the command as he struck the general with the hot iron just under the rib cage. The rod made a sharp slapping sound followed by a brief sizzle as the flesh was slightly seared under the attack. Nathan withheld a full scream but let out a muffled grunt of pain. After the pain subsided, Nathan did what he knew he had to in order to prevent this from being prolonged.

"No." He stated the word flatly to the dungeon master before him. The same as he had done the day prior, and the same he would do tomorrow. His next twenty minutes were a flurry of pain and questions.

"Where is the log book!?" The dungeon master would scream at his prisoner while driving the hot iron into an unused portion of the prisoner's body.

"No!" The general would shout back.

"Why was the *Havoc* in Ebb?" More flesh seared.

"No!"

"Why is there no evidence in the Ebb communication logs of your transmissions?" The sound of iron impacting flesh filled the room.

"No!"

As the session ended, Nathan was sobbing softly from the pain that had been inflicted upon him. He had read stories of war heroes who had endured torture with a grim smile and a request for more, but he knew those were fairy tales to impress children. Real torture was physically, emotionally, and mentally draining. The shouting matches and constant flow of questions had been weakening his hold on what he said, but he did manage to gain information from these sessions. He knew that the person that was having this done to him had left trails that could trace these actions. He also knew that the log book on his ship and the one at the central command did not match, but it was odd that they wanted his book so badly. They could just claim Nathan had doctored his own log to fit their story, why would they need the book itself? *Unless, the person I spoke to had felt something was going wrong and escaped with their book.* It was a possibility. In training for the record keeping part of his job, he was trained to understand that the log books belonged to the Judges, and therefore any tampering of the records would reflect personally against the note taker regardless of orders. If the person he spoke to figured out the log would be doctored or destroyed, it would be the duty of that person to safely bring the log to the Judges. *The Judges must already have the other log, so I just have to get my log to them to clear this up.*

The tension on the chains holding Nathan's hands went slack, allowing Nathan the ability to walk around the room he was held within. A small panel on the door was slid open, and a tray of food was sent inside the room. It was a couple of short ceramic bowls that had been previously broken and stuck back together with adhesives. One of the bowls contained a runny mixture of some sort of boiled grain with chopped carrots and a few pieces of an unidentifiable meat strewn throughout. The other was a bowl of water that had been slowly leaking its contents onto the wooden tray. Nathan quickly drank the water, so as not to lose any more of it, and then slowly ate the food. While eating, he utilized the light that was coming in from the small barred window on the door to examine his room again. Four walls, a wooden frame in one corner with straw thrown inside it to sleep on, and a bucket in the other corner to use as a toilet. The bucket was supposed to be changed daily, but the extended torture of a victim required postponing that changing to a once a week schedule. The chains that held Nathan by the wrists were connected to some sort of mechanism that ran into the ceiling at the center of the room. Nathan inspected each link of the chains, before settling on a pair of links that were two feet from his wrists. These links had small scratch marks where they had been tooled by a small sharp object. It had been tooled by the nail Nathan pulled from the bed frame. Nathan sat alone in his room and worked at the chain links on his arms, determined to free himself in time to rescue his city.

Nights in Ebb were usually peaceful. While some merchants did arrive late for docking, the majority of the Merchant District was shut down after dark. The streets were quiet and mostly emptied. Richard took a rare quiet moment from his busy schedule to wander the streets of the district. He had been planning his events for such a long time, which he could no longer remember what his goals had been before. He had joined the military young with the intention of being a tech mage, but his low affinity for gears prevented him from getting through the basic training, and he was reassigned to the Ebb State Defense. While a part of the state forces, he met many judges and nobles. He rubbed elbows with the largest land owners, and he spoke with the most influential of the high class. He had truly lived the high life, but he had seen the horrors of the Outer Ring first. His first assignment had been on the Outer Ring.

Richard stopped at a bakery that was still open for a bread roll that had a fruit paste baked into the center. It was already cold when he bought it due to the late time of the order, but it still had a delightful taste to Richard. This was not the first cold roll he had eaten in his life. While on the Outer Ring, it was common for the guards to purchase these rolls on the way to the edge of the city. Richard used to eat his fresh after buying it, but that had changed when he met some of the Outer Ring citizens. Their lives had an effect on his own that he never would have believed beforehand. The squalor they lived in made him feel guilty for the privilege of a clean home. Their meals made him sorrowful for taking advantage of fresh foods. He did not understand how these creatures could put on smiles and work through the day in the state that they lived. Yet, these baffling creatures would greet him happily as he passed and thank him for his service. They were grateful that he stood on a wall and would chat with him to help pass the time. They were not the scum that filtered off of the rest of the city, but the strong foundation that held the city in place, and Richard felt a deep hatred develop for the creatures that would purposefully deny these people their daily needs. It was during this time in Richard's life that luck intervened in his own plotting. As a young man standing on the wall, Richard would plot the route he would need to take to bring better living conditions to these citizens. He had planned to leave the military after his tour of service and become a judge. He would represent all of the citizens and bring a new wave of prosperity to those that did not have it, but his plans changed after a raid.

It was closer to sunset when Richard had first seen the enemy sneaking in. At first he believed them to be citizens, but they were armed, and Richard was trained to take them as dangerous. With a few other guards, Richard had confronted the sneaks, and found a group of seven people, five males and two females, that were armed with short curved swords. Upon discovery, they had immediately taken hostages using some of the children that had been roaming nearby, but...

Richard paused his memory to enjoy a bite of his roll. What came next was always the worst part, and at the time Richard had gone along with it to carry out his duty. The events haunted him now, as distant ghosts that would not find peace.

The guards that were with Richard ran the sneaks through by piercing wherever they could. For some, it was almost a sport to see if they could hit the vitals of both the child and the captor, but for Richard it was an attempt to stab without hitting the captive. In the end, seven captors had died and were confirmed to have been spies from Nenva that were there to raid Ebb for gears, but five of the children had also been stabbed, and the guards were working to silence their cries of pain. Richard stood horrified at the end of the events, and assured himself that it was just these guards that were this awful. He could not allow this disregard of life to remain, and thus he changed his plans. He worked hard to make his presence known within the military, becoming a favorite of the generals and judges until he began receiving promotions. Each rung climbed would allow him to force his subordinates to change their views of human lives. He found others like himself, strong leaders with compassion for the citizens, and began to recruit them into his ring of confidants. He rolled over the military like a wave of change until he was stationed as the High General of Ebb. It was there he found that he could go no further. Though the military was not allowed to treat anyone as a second class citizen, there was no realistic way to prevent that treatment when the citizens of the Outer Ring were second class citizens. Richard needed the judges to assist his plans for changing the entire methods of the city itself.

Richard had wandered to the Second Ring and approached a gate in the middle of the road with a mansion behind it. The guard at the gate stepped forward and halted Richard's approach.

"Halt! Who goes there?" The guard questioned.

"High General Richard Sane." Richard responded.

"Sir!" The guard changed his posture to a salute to the general before him.

"At ease."   Richard's response was well trained, and had no hostility in the words. Of course the guard knew who he was, but it was his job to question anyway. Richard was pleased to know that the guard at night was taking his job seriously. Inside the compound, Richard was greeted by his chief interrogator, the lone judge that had agreed to Richard's plan. The rest could not be trusted, as they only held value in power and money, but this person, this Judge Beverly Charles, had the same vision as he had. It was a vision of peace and enlightenment.

"Rick. A pleasure to see you. What brings you here on this cold night? Won't the wind chill your old bones?" Beverly teased with a grin. She was a slightly thicker woman with the same tan skin as most of the citizens of Ebb. Her hair was a raven black braid that fell between her shoulder blades. Her light brown eyes and slightly wrinkled face smiled at the general with delight. She held a cup with a dark liquid in one hand, and a clipboard, with different papers attached to it, in the other hand.

"My bones will be fine, Bev. How is the prisoner?" There was not concern in Richard's voice, as he did not care for those that actively worked against him.

"He is alive, but is unwilling to talk. He has been well trained, but we have gotten some information from him. From the way he has been behaving, we know that his log book still exists and is in the city. He must have allies that are hiding it, so it must be one of the people released from his ship." Beverly calmly analyzed Nathan's actions during the interrogation. She had done this before and had gained a strong insight into the things that motivate actions.

"One of the prisoners? We did clear them all for release, but that was mostly to appease the judges during the capture of a high profile general. To bring them back into custody would accelerate the plan and defeat the need for the log book. It would also cause a lot of unnecessary collateral damage, so it is not an option to just round them all back up." The two walked through the compound while talking, stopping at an office near the front.

"You don't have to round them up, let my team do that. All I need from you is a copy of the release statement, so we know who we are collecting." Beverly sat her clipboard and drink at her desk before turning back towards Richard.

"Fine, but if something happens..." Richard started, but was cut off by Beverly.

"Then we are an independent operation that was carrying out secret missions for Nenva. We'll be careful. Now go home, Rick, and get some sleep. You look like hell."

"I will. Let me know when the others have been collected. I want this whole thing finished as quickly and quietly as possible." The two shared a friendly hug before Richard left Beverly to her work. He was patient before, and he could continue to be so.

The night was getting colder as Richard went back home, a sign that the harvest would come soon.

In a farm on the northern edge of Ebb's territory, a young man was returning home for the night. He had worked hard all day and enjoyed a late night of gambling with some friends before returning home for the night. He was eager to see his child and wife, despite the current argument over the crops for the year. They were not wealthy, but they were not poor either; however, tonight the man saw his wife's point that they might have more money if he did not gamble with his friends so much. Yet, the man smiled all the same as he went home with an empty wallet and an empty stomach. His joy abruptly ended as he made it home. The lights were on inside in the middle of the night.

"Damn, what is she mad about this time?" The man asked himself, while he stood on the doorstep deciding if it was too late at night to return to his friend's house to sleep. As he shuffled around on the doorstep, he detected a noise coming up from the field. A panic swept over the man, and he swiftly opened the door to get inside. He did not consider himself a coward, but a wolf at night was more than a match for an unarmed farmer, and he had heard rumors of a pack of wolves that had been scouring the area. Some of the farms further north had been abandoned, or the residents were found dead and partially eaten by the wolves. He would take the angry wife over certain death any day.

"I'm home, dear." The man called out to the other room as he removed his shoes and coat, but he received no answer. As he rounded the corner, the reason for her silence hit the man with the weight of the world. There she lay on their living room floor in a pool of her own blood. The man stood in horror, almost incapable of pulling his eyes away from the scene. He had known her since his youth and always knew she would be his wife. He had sworn to love her until death, but found that death had not quieted his love.

When the man was capable of pulling his eyes away, he spotted a group of armored men sitting at his table with a map before them. There were five of them at the table, all wearing a grey set of steel plate mail. The men in front of the farmer were towering giants, easily a foot taller than the average Ebbian and twice abroad. Their hair colors were lighter toned than the common dark brown, and their skin was without the natural tan common in Ebb. They each had a rifle with a bayonet attached to the end hanging from the chair that they sat upon, and they wore a half cloak that was draped on them like a sash. The cloaks bore the symbol of the Nenvian Army. They sat there watching the man, gaging his reaction to the scene before him. A shorter man, compared to his comrades, sat at the head of the table, and for a moment he locked eyes with the farmer. The short man had no malice or hate in his green eyes, but a look of a man that was engaging in a negotiation or a trade deal. His large bushy eyebrows were locked in a slightly curious expression, and his left hand unconsciously rubbed a large patch of scarred skin mixed with red stubble on his neck. The short man waited to see what the farmer did after intruding upon his own home. He was testing the survival instincts of the Ebbian people.

"Who are you?" The farmer asked.

"A dead man does not need to know." The short man responded flatly. The farmer had failed his test, and had sought immediate answers instead of retreating. The farmer had been watching the scene from the doorframe, and a noise beside him caused him to turn in time to see two of the Nenvian guards coming at him with the bayonets on their rifles. He managed to grab one of the bayonets, cutting his hands in the process, but was stabbed in the chest with the other one. As the pain of the wound reached him, his hands unconsciously let go of the bayonet he had caught, and the other guard finished his thrust, stabbing the farmer in the head. It did not take long for the farmer to bleed out.

"A shame bystanders have to die for this war." One of the other commanders at the table noted, as the farmers body was thrown on top of his late wife's body.

"No," the short man began, "the only shame in war is that it was started. Everything else that occurs is just a part of the war itself and falls into the overall shame of the event. This man and his family were not bystanders in this war. These people were complacent participants that have helped to jeopardize the future of Nenva, and they are only the beginning of what we are here to accomplish." As the short man finished his speech, he heard a small noise in the hallway that lead to the bedrooms. All the men looked over to see a small girl standing in the hall beside a table she had just bumped into. Her eyes showed the terror she had witnessed, and her legs were locked in place out of fear.

"Now this is a shame," the other commander stated, "but we can't have witnesses, and we should not leave orphans." The other commander snapped his fingers, and before the night had ended, a third body had been stacked into the pile, as the soldiers from Nenva continued planning their assault on Ebb.

INVESTIGATION

In the nights of Ebb, news did not travel, and the events that occurred in the farmlands rarely made it beyond the Outer Ring of Ebb, thus the women began their investigation without any information of the growing assault on the city. From the growing unrest, talk of a curfew had spread in the Inner and Second rings, but had not been put into place, so the women walked with confidence in their plan. They started with reconnaissance by having Marla and Beth wander around the area the wall covered. Beth had been chosen for this part due to her guard equipment reducing any questioning she might otherwise receive. She marched properly around the walls nearby and paid attention to openings to find the gate. When she found the opening, she signaled to Marla by reflecting light at her with a spear. Marla was dressed in a large cloak to cover her wing mail that she had dawned for the mission. With the wing mail, the women had intended for Marla to fly above the compound and report how many guards were on watch.

Uneasiness built within Marla when Beth sent her the signal. She knew the wing mail was designed to fly. She knew which gears would play the role and the order to activate them. What she was unsure of was her own talent to lift herself. As she stood there giving herself a pep talk and going over the gears in her head, Beth sent another signal to her. *Now or never.* Marla told herself as she opened the cloak to allow it to fall between the wings. She spread the wings open in a grand flourish, stretching every bladed feather to remove the cramps she could feel through the metal. Her wings lifted towards the sky in a swift motion. She held her breath, and sent the wings crashing towards the ground while activating her gears. Just before the wings crashed into the ground beneath her feet, she lifted into the sky over the tops of the buildings. She felt the chill of the air around her, unhindered by buildings and lamps, and spread her wings to hover in place. She bobbed a bit in the air, but the design adjusted to keep her afloat. The wing mail wanted to fly, to be free from the confines of the ground. She could feel the will of the wings commanding her to dance amongst the clouds and enjoy the freedom of the air while joy rushed through her body, but Marla fought to control herself. *After the mission. After we find out who is trying to tear this city apart, then I will fly amongst the clouds.* She made this promise to herself, but she also promised the wing mail.

With her position above the compound, and her high powered lift gear, Marla swooped above the hidden building and scanned the area by feeling the surface with her lift gear. Every trip above the compound gave more information, as her gear slipped inside the windows, under the cracks of doors, and between bars. The effort made Marla nauseous and gave her a headache that felt as though a lead ball had been crammed into her skull. She made emergency landings beside Beth several times in order to complete the mission, each time resting for a little while longer before regaining the ability to take off. The strain was immense, as the lead ball in her mind had begun to fill her entire body from within, and the cold took her body from outside. When all the information had been passed to the others, Marla was forced to excuse herself for a while to catch her breath, warm herself, and put a stop to her mind's raging from the overwork. Beth, Digit, and Debra puzzled over the information that was provided during this time.

The building was formerly a hospital or hotel based on the number of rooms that were present in the building. The upper floors seemed to be offices, but the only evidence for this assumption was the inclusion of a table and chair in each of the rooms. The night staff seemed to number in the double digits somewhere between 25 to 50 people. Marla had found it difficult to identify the number of people in a group if they were in the same room, as the lift gear was not designed to tell objects apart. She had found it even harder to tell if a person was sitting at one of the desks or not, as the gear identified the entire object as a chair or a table in her mind. The women chose to take a high estimate and assume there were 50. Marla also noted the building had a subsection, but it was outside of the reach of her lift gear to tell what was down there.

While Marla had been flying around the building, Beth had wrapped up her own mission as well, by observing the patrol routes and methods of the guards. She had even managed to get close enough to listen to a conversation between a couple of the guards. It was not much to go on, but Beth had a hunch that these people were not associated with the military. The problem with this theory was the uniforms the men wore matched the EAF Special Forces. The women determined that this building was a private military compound that was owned by someone with access to the EAF's equipment and training. With the initial investigation part done, the women had to decide what to do with this information.

"We cannot do anything with what we have. We have no evidence that this building is not a military building, nor can we prove that this has anything to do with the growing unrest between the military and the Judges." Beth spoke up first with a practical tone. "This building has secret base written all over it, and if someone were trying to do illegal things, this would be the ideal location for it. No one knows it exists. We have to do something about this information." Debra rebutted.

"Beth is right, we can't act with only what we have. If there is a conspiracy to pit the guards against the military, we still have nothing proving a connection with this building. Maybe it is time to call it quits and turn over any information we have to the Judges." Marla stumbled over to the group from her resting place, her wing mail keeping her standing.

"Or," Digit chimed in, "we sneak in through the wall joint between the main city wall and the branching point. Those junctions usually have trash piled nearby, and a few of them have boards placed beside houses for scaling walls." The rest of the women looked at Digit with a slight nod. Surely they had each seen trash piled by the walls before, but the inclusion of decent boards in trash piles was never something they had looked for. Only a person who had helped plant such boards, no doubt stolen from construction warehouses, or people that had stolen their way into the Inner Rings would need to know about such a feature. As trash disposal was often left to a select team from the Outer Ring to deal with, it seemed likely to the other women that Digit's words could be true.

"That would certainly make it easier to climb up the walls, so let's go see if we are lucky tonight." Debra responded. Beth and Marla exchanged a worried glance that shared a silent understanding of the situation they were in. A secret compound that is posing as the military could easily make people disappear.

"Why don't we just skip the building and look for the skulker like we originally planned?" Marla asked again.

"I know something is going on in Ebb, and after seeing the secrecy of this place, I'm fairly certain this building has evidence of what's going on. If I'm right, then we don't have to stop them from doing anything, we just have to turn in any information we get to the Judges and let the state handle it. If I'm wrong, the worse punishment you receive for illegal entry into a private building is a few months in the prison or a fine. I know the skulker is important to Digit, we've all seen the way her eyes light up when we got new reports, but Ebb is important to all of us, and we have to work to protect it from itself." Debra gave her reasoning to Marla in a hushed but certain tone, showing her dedication to this cause.

"Let us all remain cautious." Beth said to the group, but looked intently at Debra as she said it, "We are only here to gather information." Debra responded with a large grin and grabbed

Beth's right hand with both of her own.

"Of course." Debra reassured her friend before letting go of her hand, leaving Beth staring absently at her right hand for a moment. "Now, let's go!"

The women silently stole their way across the emptied roads, taking care to avoid the light of the oil lamps that burned on the corners of the streets. Digit broke away from the rest of the women, with the intent to rejoin them at the wall after she had found a board. The quiet world around them hid their intentions as they arrived at the corner wall surrounding the compound. The location of choice fell behind a few shops that had been abandoned for years. Their windows had been boarded up to replace the shattered glass of some ancient event, and none of the women could recall ever seeing these buildings in operation. They sat lonely by the corner of the wall, covering the activities of the poor members of society like silent guardians. Now these buildings watched over the intrepid women as they waited patiently for Digit to return to them with a means of entering the hidden compound.

By the time Digit returned with a large enough plank for scaling the wall, the night had grown cold as time shifted into a new day. Beth, Debra, and Digit used the plank to cross over the wall, while Marla used her wing mail to leap over. After dragging the board over as well and hiding it in some nearby foliage, the women examined the courtyard for an entrance into the manor. The yard at eye level was flat and grassy, with hints of color dancing under the lights on the wall, as the last of the fireflies paraded around for their final hurrah before their season ended. Across the grass was the side of the manor, shrouded in darkness with no light shining from within. Even the late night workers seemed to have abandoned the building and retired for the night. The women moved as silently as they could across the yard and positioned themselves under a window that opened into a room that appeared to be a study. Small bits of light that streaked into the windowed revealed bookcases and chairs in the room and a door towards the center of the building with light coming in from the cracks.

Marla gave the others a silent questioning gaze and pointed at the window. Debra eagerly nodded her head. Debra then looked to Beth, before pointing at her and then the ground, indicating Beth to keep watch. Marla focused her wing mail's lift gear at the lock on the inside of the window. Lift gear was not capable of going through solid objects, but a strong enough gear could squeeze through the cracks of doorways and window frames. Marla knew her gear could do this from the first time she had called out to it. She also knew she would need to bring herself back into that state of desperation to push enough power into the gear to squeeze through a window frame. In her mind she called upon the memories of the ship, soaking herself in that feeling of helplessness that had once brought her to madness. She felt the window in front of her with the gear, and began groping the edges for a space to push through. When she found a proper spot, Marla pushed her mind through the crack, giving her the feeling that she had momentarily cracked her own head open. The other women watched as Marla grunted from the strain, as the lock clicked and the window raised up.

Marla let out a sigh of relief and sat upon the ground, calming her emotions before proceeding. An uneasiness descended upon her from the wing mail. The wing mail had willed her to smash the window open and take what she wanted by force. The desire to not suffer still ran strong in her body, and she fought herself to keep the wings from expanding. The other women allowed Marla to calm down before proceeding into the mansion.

By the time the women had started their mission, Richard had already made his way back to the office. Though his mind was tired and his body demanded rest, he still had one more mission to accomplish today. One more loose end to tie up before he could relax. On his way to the office, Richard had ordered his captive brought before him. When his captive was brought before him,

Richard could not help but smile. Before him stood Matthew in his full regalia, complete with the sword still by his side.

"Why did you not disarm a prisoner?" Richard knew the answer without asking.

"Sir," the guard looked at Matthew's sword as if for the first time before replying, "I failed to notice the weapon on his side. I have no excuse." Richard smiled at the guard, catching him by surprise. "Do not blame yourself. The nature of that gear blade is to prevent people from taking it. I will take over the interrogation from here. Leave us." Richard responded to the confused guard.

"Sir that would be a breach in protocol that I am not entitled to do. The prisoner is under my jurisdiction and care until the time of his trial." The guard's reply lacked any authority, but was driven by his sense of duty.

"The trial is a private one that will be watched over by me. The forms for the acceptance of the prisoner into court custody have already been filled out and are there on my desk. Turn in your paperwork back at your post and consider yourself relieved of the charge of watching this prisoner." Richard waved his hand over a short stack of signed papers on his desk. The guard accepted the papers, reviewed them for accuracy, and left the room in a hasty fashion. "Now then, why don't you have a seat?" Richard turned his attention to Matthew.

"What crime have I committed that is so great that the highest ranking general of Ebb would personally preside over it?" Matthew worded the question carefully as he sat down in the offered seat. A quick survey of the room he was in gave him two exits available. The first was through the door he came in, which would lead him into the heart of a military base. *No go.* The other exit was the window behind the general, which looked out over the city of Ebb. Being led into this base through tunnels in the Grand Market, Matthew had lost track of his exact location, but he now figured he was roughly half way up the spire.

"Straight to the point. I like that. You could be tried for treason against Ebb for stealing the *Daisy*. The penalty is death, of course."

Richard replied in a cold manner, as if speaking to a corpse.

"I'm innocent. I was sleeping in the Outer Ring when that ship was stolen." Matthew responded while examining the desk before him. *It is probably heavy considering the design.* Matthew noted while considering if he could use the desk as part of his escape. The desk currently had nothing on top of it, providing Matthew with few options to distract the man before him. The rest of the office was kept in a tidy fashion, with no extra furnishings aside from the necessities. *Guess I only have myself and the chair I'm sitting on to make it to that window.*

"Now there is no need to get worked up. I believe in making deals and working with people." The general smiled and placed his hands on the desk. He was holding no weapons, and had nothing to protect himself against an armed opponent.

"What kind of deal?" Matthew questioned in response. He was trying to determine if the man before him was trying to build trust between them, or showing Matthew that he was completely without fear.

"That's the spirit," Richard responded with a pleased tone before continuing, "I have an eye for people with talent and believe that talent should be fostered and grown. Though the penalty for treason is death, the penalty for theft is far less severe, and there is no penalty for undercover operations. Now, what level of cooperation are you willing to go with?" Matthew stared in silence for a moment, trying to get a feel of the man before him. Instinct took over, and the gear at his side produced a silent glow. It was reading, learning whatever it could about the man in front of him, but it gained nothing of intention or emotion. The general's mind was devoid of emotion.

"I would prefer not to die, and I'm not cut out for prison life. Let's discuss the idea of me working this one through." Matthew relented.

"Good choice. The world is changing, Mr. Flint, as the world always will. The Nenvian are constantly pushing the border, preparing for war and searching for an edge against our gears. At home, the Judges have grown into a private club filled with corruption and dynasties. The merchants rule the world. They pay the salaries of the military and the guard, preventing even those that should defend the people from acting their parts. Ebb festers like an infected sore, while brave men die in the wastes of the Outer Ring. I intend to fix all of those issues with a peaceful transition of power away from the Judges and onto the military. After the corruption has been ousted, and the opportunity has been spread properly among the entirety of the nation, I will cede the power of the state back over to the people. Do you have any questions?" Richard gave his explanation in the same cold fashion.

"Where do I fit into all this? You already have the military under control, and the guard seems to be ill equipped to mount any proper defense against your forces. On top of that, the border was secure enough to catch a small ship from escaping. Why did you bring me in?" Matthew asked his question carefully, still trying to pry information from this silent man.
"You are not wrong on most of those points, and my plan will work with or without your assistance. What I need from you is your control over the gear blade that you hold. You wield it on your side so casually, calling its powers in a moment's notice, but you probably are unaware at what a rare feat that is. Gearsmiths attain a master rank by being capable of building gears that anyone can use, but their true talent lies in the creation of the gear mail that is utilized by the military. Gear mail is usable due to the contact that they make with the person holding it. The stronger the ability, the more of the person it has to touch, so fire mails coat the entire torso and mortar mails have to include the neck and legs. Some people; however, have an affinity to gears and can use even the most powerful of gears with little to no contact. Your use of that blade is a testament to your natural born talent. Should you have been born or raised anywhere but the Outer Ring, you would have been a fine gear mage. I want you to use that blade to extract

information from a reluctant adversary in order to prevent radical militant forces from emerging during the takeover. I want this takeover to be as merciful as possible." Richard moved his fingers together as he spoke, bringing the tips of his middle fingers to his chin and resting his elbows on the desk.

"So the deal you mentioned. I get you the information you want from some guy, and you wipe my record clean? What about the *Daisy*?" Matthew grew bold from the explanation that he was not needed but wanted.

"Yours. We will repair the *Daisy* and hand it over to you as captain. Afterwards, you can decide if you want to remain under my command or flee the city and live in exile. Do we have a deal?" Richard extended his right hand forward. Matthew took no time during his deliberation, and extended his own hand out to meet the general's.

"Deal."

SANE'S PLOY

A night guard of Ebb looked out towards the empty fields beyond the Outer Wall. The new moon brought darkness to the world, keeping all the houses that slept hidden in the night. The guard kept a rough blanket wrapped around his torso to fight off the advancing cold nights that heralded in the end of summer. On most nights of this time, the guard expected to keep a peaceful watch, but tonight felt different. He saw lights that remained on all night for the past few nights. These lights seemed to have a pattern that led them closer to the gate. They had started a week prior in a small village that was just within sight of the wall. Now that village did not seem to sleep, and the guards were on alert for trouble. They did not suspect Nenvian soldiers this deep into Ebb's territory. They could not suspect such an event to occur. There were check points and fortresses between Ebb and the border. Though General Omar had been taken into captivity, his post was filled by a general handpicked by High General Sane. The norther border of Ebb was secured.

Yet, the guards on the wall felt something was going to happen, and the peace in which the Ebbian people had thrived under was going to be threatened. With this feeling of unease, the guards stood on the wall in a much larger number than usual. They hid their numbers within the shadows of the ramparts and cramped within small guard houses. The night guard of Ebb stood in full force on the northern wall, prepared to fight whatever enemy was approaching the city. A loud sound broke the stillness of the night, and the projectile that struck one of the guards caused him to sound the alarm with an undignified scream of pain. The

Nenvians had come for battle.

The north wall quickly lit up with the lights of the guards' shield gears and torches. The next round of bullets were suspended in the air by the power of the lantern shaped shield gears, as a faint wave of white luminescence spread between the guards and an undertone of blue light lit up at their feet. The towers that stood on the ramparts began to light up, and spot lights began to aim out towards the attackers, as the guards were attempting to find a target to fire at. While the inner city guards used spears to keep the peace, the outer city guards were given soft lighting gears to deter intruders. While the soft lighting gears did not pack the same punch as the standard lightning gear used by the gear mages, they were simple enough for anyone to use and could be mass produced. The blue glow at the feet of the guards was the light of the gears charging up to be used. The moment the spot light revealed an enemy, the wall crackled and reached out with a tendril of lightning at the invader on the ground, burning him to death in an instant and igniting his gear. The light from the burning corpse revealed more invaders hidden in the darkness, and the crackling tendril of lightning began to shift and dance along the ground where enemies lay hidden. The sound was deafening as booms of thunder hurled across the northern wall, and the flashing lights were blinding to those not properly prepared. The ear covers meant to protect the guards' ears, the glasses made to protect the guards' eyes, and the commotion of the fight allowed a team of the Nenvians to cross the wall undetected and enter into the city. The wolves at the gate were now among the flock within.

The Nenvians at the wall began to retreat backwards, their time limit for the infiltration being met. It was a slow crawl away from the front line, with any soldier that strayed even a little above the ground being torched by the wall for being careless. The commanders waited in suspense for the return of their troops. Though the mission they were on was the highest priority for the Kingdom of Nenva, the military had been trained to value the life of a soldier. These men were not drafted but chosen. They were chosen to serve the greatest honor in the kingdom, but they were alive like any other. They had wives and children, and the commanders wanted to bring all of them home. The reunion of the troops was a joyous and solemn time. Out of the five thousand chosen for this mission, four hundred were dead or missing. The most chilling issue the soldiers saw was the amount of people who had been wounded but lived was zero. The men sat hidden inside the houses of the Ebbian farmers stone faced, considering the danger of the gears they were facing and praying to their God for the success of their brethren who had infiltrated the city.

The team chosen to infiltrate the walls wore clothing stolen from the farmhouses and were armed with one six shot revolver and knife each instead of rifles. Five groups of five individuals began to spread out into the city, each team set to its own objective. Nenvians did not look like the Ebbian people they were invading, so the teams had taken precautions before entering, and the attack was done at night to increase the chance of success. They had smudged their faces with dirt to draw attention away from the distinct lack of bronze coloring and walked hunched over in large clothing. In the Outer Ring the disguise held, but as the different groups approached the second wall, they found themselves under increased scrutiny. With the stealth and cunning of trained special operatives, the five teams combined back together outside of the main objective, a mansion in the Second Ring with the walls wrapped around it. The Nenvians double checked their maps to confirm the location before storming inside the building, catching the two guards at the entrance flat footed and deftly removing them from the potential threat list. They were here on a mission and could not tolerate any delays or errors. They would infiltrate this manor and find their target. They would kill anyone that got between them and their target. They would escape with their target. They were the Nenvian elites, and they would not fail here. With a grim expression, twenty five Nenvian elites entered the manor from the front door. The men quickly silenced the staff in the main room and inspected the manor before them. A living space on the bottom floor with bedrooms at the top of a grand staircase. The teams checked the study and kitchen first, being closest to the front door before moving towards the ballroom and bedrooms above. The main hall of the building was an open floor that went up to the roof with a large staircase and hanging walkway leading to the bedrooms above the kitchen and study. The ballroom occupied a quarter of the house and stretched up to both floors, with a balcony on the second level for sitting and a slightly raised stage for a band to play. Behind the stage was a fireplace large enough to walk inside of. The teams converged on the fireplace and found it to be clean of any soot or residue despite the roaring flame that appeared to be burning. One of the members reached towards the flame and surprised the rest of the elites when his hand met a curtain. The fire that burned was behind the curtain and a staircase that led down into the basement.

Behind the elites, the women had wandered into the manor. While they silently checked the study, the marauders hunted in the hallways. As Digit cautiously peered through the door, the Nenvians silently shifted towards the hidden staircase. Now it was the locals' turn to check the recently emptied manor for clues or news. In the kitchen, the group found sufficient supplies to house roughly twenty guests for an extended stay, but the bedrooms that they searched indicated that no one had been living in this building. There were no personal items of any sort displayed within the building, as even the books were seemingly made up entirely of reference books, and the entire house seemed to be coated in a thin layer of dust from lack of use.. A muffled conversation amongst the women provided no answers to the issue.

"It could be a hideout for the merchants." Marla proposed.

"The merchants came after the construction of the wall, they couldn't have built this place." Debra remarked.

"That would indicate the Judges have something to do with this place." Beth noted.

"Maybe it is a secret testing facility where they are trying to make mutated monsters to battle the Nenvians." Digit chimed in, excitement building within her at the possibilities of this building. A smile covered her features as she spoke with wide eyes that searched for more. Being from the Outer District, she never had time to dream of more than a full stomach and a soft bed, now she was in a secret building trying to unravel its mysteries. She had long since forgotten the original reason she had come inside. Before long, the group had made it to the room farthest from the entrance, the ballroom.

"Whoever built this place appears to have built it to house private parties." Beth commented as she ran her fingers over a desk. Her features shifted very slightly towards confusion as she pulled back clean fingers. Her comrades failed to notice her tension as her eyes scoured the room.

"I bet the parties this room has seen were filled with the richest of merchants and most important of Judges." Debra commented as she stared at the grand fireplace. She was entranced by the smoky colored bricks and the warmth that was coming from the fire. Beth noticed the fire as well, and the distinct lack of adequate heating coming from a lit fireplace.

"We are not alone." Beth paused as she spoke, causing the others to tense up from the sudden statement. She pointed towards a place on the curtain that had snagged when the Nenvians had previously gone through. Digit was the first to step forward, excitement filling her movements, before Beth gently caught her shoulder to stop her. Beth could feel tension hanging over the mansion. Goosebumps formed on her skin, she felt her heartbeat speed up a step, and her senses sharpened as adrenaline began to rush through her. In her heightened state, she heard the sound of conflict faintly in the distance beyond the curtain. "Now might be the time to turn back."

"Why? What happened?" Debra asked quietly, sensing the dread that was building within her friend.

"I heard metal striking stone beyond that curtain." Beth replied, listening for any more clues in the unbroken silence beyond the veil. Marla pushed the curtain aside to reveal the staircase beyond. "Give me a moment, and I'll see what is happening down there." Marla spoke quietly as well, as her wing mail began to hum. Without the added stress of remaining in flight, the scan was fairly easy for Marla to accomplish. She felt her mind wander down the spiral staircase built of large stone blocks. She unconsciously prodded the cracks for hidden rooms as her mind passed by. The basement she came to consisted of a large open room with objects spaced in short intervals along the walls, and a few randomly placed objects laying upon the floor. There were three doors attached to this room, all open, and hallways beyond the doors. Her mind shifted down the hallways one at a time, each hallway causing a look of strain to cross her features as she overextended her view. With this search, she found a hallway filled with barred rooms and two sets of living people bunkered down against one another. Marla felt conflict, and the wing mail reacted. *Marla.* Her vision of the event changed from a questionable blur with outlines of objects, to a clear movie playing in her head in slow motion. *Marla.* She could see the sides aiming at each other with lightning gears and a small weapon with a barrel that she had never seen before. *Marla!* It launched projectiles at high speed towards the other people, and Marla felt an air of superiority ripple through her knowing the wing mail could handle the entire barrage with ease.

"Marla!" The voices brought her mind back to her body. Digit, Beth, and Debra were holding onto her while standing in the entrance to the staircase.

"There is a fight going on downstairs. Two different groups are going at each other, one with lightning and lift gears, the other with a strange weapon I've never seen before. They were fighting in front of a prison." Marla casually explained what she saw, trying to draw attention away from her loss of control.

"That prison is likely to hold the reason we are here." Debra responded with certainty. The women knew they were after a reason for the recent lockdown, and a hidden prisoner in a non-existent building should be able to shed light on the situation.

"Maybe Matthew is down there." Digit joined in with renewed hope.

"If we head down this staircase, we will need to be careful

of encountering hostiles. Though they are battling each other, there is little evidence suggesting either of them are allies to us." Beth took a position in front of the group as she spoke, taking the place Marla had been at. The women looked towards each other and gave a nod. Fate had brought them together, curiosity had brought them to the mansion, and now it was a sense of duty that was driving them on. They were no longer a rag tag group of women listening to gossip from the city, now they were investigators trying to find the link between the recent increases of military presence with the trauma that had befallen them. The group slowly stalked down the stairs with Beth in the lead and Marla at the end. The bottom of the stairs revealed the opening Marla had probed and presented the randomly placed objects as bodies. The room had a faint smell of blood, and the fighting in the back hall was clearly audible.

Marla felt a pulse run through her mind as she entered the room, and a single question raised in her mind. *Now what?* The problem set her mind racing for options, as she realized the group had left this part out of their plans. Beth seemed to know what she was doing, but Marla attributed that to her training and work as a guard. The rest of the women had the same confused look as Marla on their face, a confusion that was amplified by hand signals given out by Beth to the rest of the team. First, Beth raised her left hand in an open palm fashion directly above her head and pointed at it with her right. Then, Beth raised her right hand in the air and gave a number two, followed by a flat palm pointed towards the right. She then raised her left hand and made a fist, then a number one, and another flat palm pointed towards the left. After her hand signals, Beth crouched low and was about to shift along the left wall when a hand rested on her shoulder and stopped her. Beth turned around and saw Debra giving her a strange looked and slightly shaking her head.

"I know you signed instructions, but I didn't understand a single one." Debra whispered to Beth, softening Beth's hardened stare into what Debra now knew as smile. The others still could only make out the same semi blank expression that Beth always wore.

"My apologies. I fell into habit. We need to do a quick search for weapons while the residents are distracted. Two go right and one go with me left." Beth clarified in a hushed tone and proceeded left with Debra following behind her.

Marla and Digit quickly looked through the halls on the right side while trying to keep their ears and eyes open for the fighting in the hall to cease. The rooms on the right indicated this facility was some type of training ground, with a room with fifty beds, a stocked kitchen and pantry, and an open room with a floor mat in the middle. Old lightning gears that barely sparked and slightly busted wooden weapons and armor indicated this room would have been used for sparring and weapon training. Across from the training room was a locked door. A quick mental test proved the lift gears would not be able to get around the door and unlock it from the inside, so Marla raised her right wing in a striking position, ready to punch the door in, before she was stopped by Digit.

"If we break the door, people will know we were here. Give me a moment and I'll get it open." Digit began working on the lock itself using her lift gear. Marla lowered her wing and watched Digit work the lock open. For a moment, Marla was surprised by Digit's skill, but a quick thought of the teen's history reminded Marla that larceny was the normal for a person living in the Outer Ring. One quick click, and the door swung open to reveal a large armory. The two girls waved their comrades over before going inside, behind the women the sounds of combat increased, indicating more soldiers had shown up from somewhere. Once all the women had made it into the room, Digit locked the door behind them.

Before the women was a large room filled with eight rows of shelves. The shelves were neatly filled with open wooden crates that revealed pieces of armor and weaponry at a glance. From the size of the room and number of crates, a small army could be raised using the equipment in the room. At the far wall of the room contained no shelves, but there were a couple of layers of closed crates stacked up neatly against the wall. Immediately to the left of the door was a mid-sized wooden desk with a small wooden stool behind it. On the desk were papers sorted into two different stacks labels as 'received' and 'shipped.' Beth walked down the middle aisle of the room and inspected some of the weapon boxes, while the other three followed Debra as she sifted carefully through the desk. She casually flipped through the receipts, being careful to not change their order, before opening the drawers on the desk. It made an audible click in a silence that had crept up so suddenly, that the women did not pay any attention to it. A broad smile crossed her face as she came across a bound notebook with a leather bound cover.

"A ledger," Debra began her explanation, "it looks like it has some recent acquisitions in it. Let's see. Some weapons checked in recently. Here they bought a large order of lightning gears from several different gearsmiths. Wow, that is a lot of food. Doesn't make sense with the amount of equipment. They have a recording of paychecks to personnel in here, but there are too many for a compound this size. It's like this place is preparing to be sieged." Debra flipped through the book, talking mostly to herself while reading over the scribbles and notes hastily drawn inside the ledger. She stopped completely when she came across an entry labeled *Daisy*. "This entry calls for repairs to the *Daisy*, but it is dates before the first launch, and the cost is left open. Approved by RS. Whoever works here planned for the *Daisy* to be stolen. What's more, it looks like they are planning an attack on Ebb."

"If they were going to do it, now would be the best time." Beth commented from the aisle. "These weapons have been recently maintained, and the only non-merchant sky ship in the dock is the *Havoc*, as the arrest of a frontier general would require the flagship of Ebb to take a position on the frontier during the trial."

"I think we should leave." Digit whispered as she noticed the silence. "Sounds like the fighting is over, and I don't want to get pinned in here." Digit had already went over to the door, ready to unlock it and scatter as years of larceny had taught her. Marla had a strange feeling as well that started at her spine as a soft tingle. The feeling then spread quickly across her back and throughout her whole body.

"Let's go then." Debra agreed, tucking the ledger into her shirt. "This should give us everything we need to find out who is the cause of this and shut it down before it consumes Ebb." Debra explained to her comrades. With a quick flick, the door was opened and the women ducked out into the hall, making a line towards the stairs. Upon their arrival in the main room, they were forced to crouch in the poorly lit hallway to avoid detection from a stream of fresh soldiers heading towards the combat zone. Beth's face went pale as she recognized several of the people from both the Ebb State Defense and the EAF. The enemy of Ebb had fully infiltrated both militaries, and the ledger Debra held had suddenly become the most important item for rooting out the internal enemies of Ebb.

"No matter what happens now, you have to get that ledger to the Judges before these people succeed in taking Ebb." Beth whispered

to Debra after the soldiers had passed. Debra gave a sorrowful look at Beth before responding.
"We have to. Not me, all of us. We are all going to get this ledger to safety, and we are all going home in the end. Don't say scary things like something out of a story. Don't you know they call those death flags?" Debra's complaints were quieted after that as another group of soldiers came into the main room, stopping between the women and the stairs to freedom. They had taken up guard posts to ensure none of the insurgents made it out, and had successfully pinned the women in as well.
"I can catch that guard by surprise long enough to get his spear and give us access to the stairwell. After that, it will be a sprint to the exit." Beth whispered her plan, while pointing out the guard closest to the hall. Marla twitched behind the others. Her eyes widened at the sight of people blocking her path. Her skin prickled at the sounds of boots stomping through the halls.
She was trapped. *I'm trapped. I'm imprisoned again. These people will hurt me.* She looked ahead for her friends, her comrades, but only saw empty shells of people with distant voices. She took a step back, involuntarily trying to escape the prison she had found herself in. Her right wing bumped into something directly behind her. Her eyes went wide and her mind went dim.
Marla's mind had cracked.

BREAKDOWN

What is happening? My heart feels like it's about to pound out of my chest, but it's almost like that heart doesn't belong to me. Am I losing my mind again? Have I already lost it? Why can't I see anything...?
Don't panic Marla, keep it together. You can pull yourself through this just like last time. You can regain control.
What was that sound? It feels like I hit something with the wing. I hope it wasn't one of the girls.
No! I won't let it be one of them. Get a grip on yourself pull through. There! I can see through my eyes now. Distantly, but vision none the less. That mark looks like I struck a wall and not a person. Good, good. Hopefully the girls have realized what is happening and will clear out of my way.
There in front of me! That's Beth! No, Beth! Dodge! Please! My vision! Let me see again! Did I hit her or did she dodge?
Ugh. This lurching feeling I do remember. I am moving. Something must have threatened me to force me to move on. Must be the guards. I have to calm down though, or I won't be able to see. Calm... Calm... Calm. Deep breaths. And... Vision is back. Looks like I am swiping at the guards from the front of the stairs. Maybe I can pull a bit more control of myself away from the wings. Come on wings, give me back my senses. Yes! I can hear again.
I can hear...
Screaming and laughter? My laughter!
What is this feeling? Joy? Am I happy? Why am I feeling this shiver of pleasure run through the back of my head with each motion of my wings? Why do I want to see more of what is under this man's skin? I can feel the motions as though I am ordering them. If I think a bit harder, can I pull back on the next one? Now that I have ripped open that man, will I be able to do less to the next... I ripped that man open... Ugh, butterflies go away and stop tying up my stomach. God, my head hurts! More are coming. This pain is getting unbearable! I count three more. Just puke already! Those look like lightning gears.

Lightning gears!

Ouch! That one shot me... Aghh! They are aiming for the wings... This smell! I see, I am healing... It's so gross! They are trying to prevent the wings from stitching me together... That hurt! They damaged the right wing... I'm tired of being hurt! Looks like I won't be able to fly with this... I'm tired of being used! My promise to the wings is broken... I'm tired of being scared! My master's final work... I'm angry! I am angry... Someone is going to pay for this! That is what this feeling is about... You are going to pay for this!

Slice them! Dice them! Rip them to shreds! Taste the blades of my wings! You are the one that hurt my right wing! Don't look at me with panicked eyes! It is too late for you! It is too late for all of you! Whoosh! Whip! Swish! I love the sound my wings make as they swing through the air! I love the freedom I'm feeling! I am free of guilt! I am free of pride! I am free of everything that tethers me to this painful world! I am the master of my own fate! Nothing is a part of my world and nothing is where I belong!

Wait! Please, don't do this. Don't make me do this. I hear it now, a voice that is not my own. A voice that has invaded my mind and is wringing away my sanity. I know that you are me and not me. I know your pain because the pain is mine, but I know that I don't want this. What about Beth? What about Debra? What about Rebecca?

What about them? Foolish, insignificant nothings that fleetingly walk the world.

No. That's wrong. I am also fleeting. We are fleeting. I know that you are the wings upon my back. I know that you are angry, but this is not the way to do things. This isn't right.

Wings? Ha! No, I am neither the wings nor some invader in my conscience. I am the herald of vengeance that is bringing my power to bear. I am me. I am Marla. Your voice is the one that is odd. Spoken in my tone and in my head, but you have no concern over what these people did. You have forgotten how everything was taken from me.

I haven't forgotten, only forgiven...

Forgiven? Forgiven! How could you forgive these people? These soldiers were directly involved in covering up my kidnapping. These soldiers did it for some agenda, some secret event that their commander is organizing.

I don't know that for sure...

I know it! I have read their minds, sifted through their memories. I have lived several lifetimes this way and seen the same results. These men did this on purpose to get money and status, and they freed that son of a bitch pirate!

I know they did, and I hid that from Rebecca. She is innocent and young, and her life has already been so wrong. She needs to move on from this part of her li...

You want to save her! She was directly responsible for the death of Alder. Don't you care? He raised me like a daughter! He showed more pride for my work than my parents ever did! He loved me, and I loved him! I wanted him to be at my wedding. I wanted him to help me train my children in the craft. Now he is dead! I haven't forgiven Rebecca. That is the reason I haven't told her about the pirate. I want her to take personal responsibility for her actions. I want her to suffer through the same loveless life she has sentenced me to live.

You're right, I don't forgive Rebecca, but Beth and Debra saved me. They got me to freedom and returned me home.

And then what did they do? I admit to having respect for Beth. She has done nothing but treat me well, and she went as far as getting injured to perform her duty, but Debra. Debra does not deserve my affection or friendship. She is nothing but a naive twit that has allowed her vision of sunshine and rainbows to plague this mission. She found that ledger, and it will free General Omar and possibly prevent this civil war from happening, but who do you think she will give it to? Do you think she is going to take it to the Judges herself? No, she will take it to her father. The man that locked eyes with me while I was being carried away and shuttered his windows in response. That was a man that knew what was happening. That is a man that knows about this strife and is supporting it.

I hadn't considered that...

Bullshit! You knew right after the kidnapping, when he did not press charges. You knew that he was in on this whole thing when his daughter was returned to him and he immediately let her wander alone again.

Debra instantly recognized the shorthand in the ledger. He is supplying these people with the arms.

And she is guilty as well. She knew where to find the ledger, because she is a part of it too. These wings will allow me to take justice and vengeance and malice into my hands and crush those that are deserving. It almost feels that this unique set of gear mail was made just for me. That this was Alder's final gift to me, so that I could use it to right the wrongs of this world.

*But if I kill indiscriminately, then I **am** the wrongs of this world. I believe Alder made these wings for me, because they called out to me.*

No one has come asking for them. No one seems to even know about them or their type. They are unusual and fantastic, and I am ruining them by killing these men. I have my senses, but it is hard to maintain with the stench of blood making me gag. The screams have finally quieted, but that only brings me more concern. What kind of monster have I become?

The kind of monster I had to be. The kind of monster that this world needs. Maybe this coup is not a bad idea. Maybe this world needs a change.

Quiet. It is time for you to be quiet again. My mind is mine. My body is mine, and these wings are mine as well. You. You are also mine. You are my rage, my justice, but you need to sleep again, because this silence is more unsettling than anything else I have encountered while in this state of mind. Quiet.

Quiet...

Marla awoke from her trance in a confused state. Her vision blurred for a moment before she could focus her eyes. Her mind still pounded with pain, but this pain was different than before. Instead of the slow buildup of stress, this was caused by the overexertion she had put on herself. She looked over her surrounding for some hints to what she had been doing, and found that she was suspended in the air by her wings, which had been acting as both feet and claws. She was in a large room with multiple bunks. The room had no furnishing, other than the beds, and was devoid of personal touches that would indicate this being a dorm. The door that had been ripped from its hinges and thrown across the room. The room had a barred window, revealing this to be a holding cell. The ground beneath Marla was drenched in blood and the body parts of the ten or twelve residents of the room that had been ripped open by a large bladed object. Her wings still dripped with some of the body parts, showing what fate had befallen them. The overload of her senses caused Marla to vomit into the pool of death below her and swiftly make an escape from this room.

Beyond the doorway, Marla found herself in an unfamiliar hallway that could only be deeper in the compound. Death had found its way here as well, as Marla found bodies that had been impaled with their own spears and pinned to the walls. The ground had met death as well, as some of the bodies had not been pinned. Confused on how one person could have caused all this damage uninjured, Marla inspected herself for wounds. Though she did not feel any pain, she did see some fresh gashes that had been closed with some sort of metallic material. With the hall in the same gruesome shape as the room she had left, Marla decided to keep using the wings as legs as she clumsily skittered down the hallway. Though she tried not to step in any of the bodies along the path, her control of the wings in this fashion was not effective. It was during this time that Marla realized she was crying. There was no screaming or bawling, but tears were rolling down her face in a gentle and steady fashion. She was sad because her late master's final work was being used in such a manner. She was sad because she had gotten herself lost while enraged. She was disappointed in herself for honestly believing that her friends deserved death by her hands. The tears rolled down her face, because she knew she would never be the same person. She had lost a piece of herself today and possibly much more. Tears rolled freely down Marla's face because she did not have the time to lose herself again, not while she did not know the status of her allies.

Marla wandered the halls lost in thought, reflecting on everything that had brought her to this point. Most of the doors in this prison had been beaten in and left splintered, broken, or bent on the ground beneath them. The few doors that were left intact seemed to have been done randomly instead of intentionally. Marla let her hand wander on one of the unmolested metal doors in a sea of destruction, and felt something strange from within the room beyond. It was a strong feeling of need, but it seemed wrong for the situation. At first, Marla felt as though the feeling was desperation. As though beyond the door was a political prisoner that had heard the ruckus outside and was trying to find any way possible to survive the onslaught, but desperation can feel very similar to another feeling that humans have. Determination.

Beyond this door was a person that was determined to stay alive and to escape. Another inspection of this door revealed it to be different from the others. This door was made entirely out of metal, with notches and marks that would normally be found on a gear, but this was no gear. This door had no feeling or presence, and Marla was unable to make a connection with it. She could not touch it with her lift gear. This was an antigear. Alder had once discussed the idea of such a thing, but he had always spoken of it as though it were a fairy tale. This was a reality that brought a moment of excitement to Marla's life and temporarily made her forget about the trauma she had been through. She ran her fingers over the grooves of the metal, studying with her eyes what she could not see with her gear, before that feeling from before swelled back into her mind. Determination.

"Hello." Marla called out to the door. She had considered leaving, considered not getting involved with some secret militaries political prisoners, but she had already done so much to this shadow organization that an ally or two would be welcome. Marla also had a sense of guilt creeping through her mind about the many dead prisoners that were directly her fault. "Hello in there." Marla called out again after a short silence.

"Hello." A male voice finally called back with a rasp.

"I'm going to get you out of this cell, so I need you to stay away from the doorway." Marla finally placed her feet on the ground and lifted her wings into an attack position. She hesitated for a moment, reluctant to destroy the beauty of an antigear, but she reminded herself that she had work to do yet and was unsure of exactly how long she had been down here. Marla swung her right wing hard into the door, ripping the door from the hinges with a snap and tearing out a piece of the wall with it. She flinched as the door was thrown halfway across the room, chiding herself for using too much force, before stepping in to find a thin man chained to the far wall, with a body covered in bruises and his left eye swollen shut. His grey hair matted against his head and grew in an awkward fashion, leaving several bald spots scattering over his head. A slight smile had found its way beyond a thick grey and black beard. His right eye was framed with a horrid scar and stared at Marla. It was a metal orb with a glowing blue pupil. Marla had found Nathan Omar.

"I recognize you. You were the girl from the *Daisy*." Nathan said while Marla set her wings against his chains.

"You remember me?" Marla responded as the chains snapped easily before the wings.

"It is hard to forget something like those. That is a unique design that likely took years to perfect. By the makers mark and detail in the grooves, I'd wager that was the work of Alder Node." Nathan's reply caught Marla by surprise.

"You knew Alder?" Marla asked, while helping Nathan to his feet. The man looked malnourished, but he still had the strength to stand on his own.

"Yeah, Alder enlisted in the EAF at the same time I did. We fought together in a few skirmishes during the first few years before I was picked for officer training and he was picked to be a gear mage candidate. After that, I heard he flunked out of the gear mage academy and became a gear smith instead. We didn't talk much after that, but he did fix my eye for me." Nathan explained while the two navigated through the corridors. Marla was about to ask more questions but was stopped by a raised hand from Nathan. "I'm sure you have a lot of questions for me, and I have a lot of questions for you as well, but let's save those for when we are clear of this hell hole."

"Right." Marla agreed uneasily. She had seen a fair amount of death this day and no longer held any certainty that anyone would survive long enough to have later conversations, but she did see the wisdom of not chatting in a graveyard and fell silent.

Outside the compound and beyond the wall sat Debra, Beth, and Digit, who were busy patching up a large scratch on Beth's stomach. Though the wound appeared gruesome, the lack of bleeding indicated it was shallow, tearing a mark through Beth's outfit and causing minor damage to the woman's clothes. The women sat in the calm of the night, paranoid by the contrast from the chaos they escaped. Luck had found their team to safety only a few hours after they first entered the compound.

"Now what do we do?" It was the thought on each woman's mind and said out loud by one of them.

CIVIL WAR

Two hours before dawn and Richard had not slept yet. His prison had been assaulted and both his valuable prisoners had escaped. Although he was not totally unprepared for this outcome, he had not anticipated this turn of events to be likely. Yet there was no frustration crossing his features. Richard stood staring out of his office window at the calm city below, marveling at the beauty the city held in the predawn hours. A few lights began to spring up in the early hours, restaurants that served breakfast preparing for the morning rush. Some other lights were from the couriers beginning to move goods through the rings for deliveries made before opening. The city as it was worked as though it was one machine. All the parts came together as though it were one of the gears it produced.

"I hope this can be seen again after today." Richard mused to himself as his eyes wandered the city basked in darkness. The break in had done little more than advance his schedule, with events that would have taken place at the end of the month taking place now. The break in also ended his desire for Matthew's help. An interrogator is not worth anything without a prisoner to interrogate, and Richard no longer had the time to bring his part of the deal to fruition. While Richard planned his next moves, his High Captain approached the office, stopping at the doorframe and delivering a sharp knock.

"Enter." Richard gave the command without turning around. He knew the gait and pattern of the knock and was expecting no other visitors. The man that entered was clean shaven and dressed in proper military attire. He held a lighting staff at attention as he centered himself in the room. In his other hand was a small stack of papers, reports from Captains spread throughout the city.

"Sir, High Captain Daniels reporting." He spoke in a measured and practiced pace. Richard turned to face the man before him, this man that was the very definition of average. Average height, average weight, brown hair, brown eyes, and tanned skin. This man had reached his rank for the ability to blend into any situation, but now Richard needed him to stand above others. Now Richard needed him to stand out.

"Report, High Captain." Richard gave a standard response and listened carefully.

"Sir, reports have arrived from the local captains. All positions are go for operation in the Inner Ring and Middle Ring. The Outer Ring positions sent notification of position, but requested additional support due to the heightened awareness the raid brought to the Ebb State Defense in the Outer Ring." High Captain Daniels gave his summary from the papers as he handed the stack to the General. Richard's review was swift, as the situation fell into his prediction.

"The request for additional support is denied. The operation commences at the first light. Ensure that our guest is properly detained before then. You are dismissed." Richard turned back to his window at these words, and the High Captain left. Despite all of his professionalism, today was the day his long held plans took shape. It was hard to not show his excitement or fear.

Matthew awoke from his sleep suddenly, his blade pulsing at his side and giving him a slight headache. In his time of owning this weapon, he had learned to use this as an early warning bell. It told him when danger lurked, and with the pulse as rapid as it was, Matthew knew he was in danger.

"Things always change at the worst times." Matthew grumbled to himself as he swiftly dressed. He had stayed through the morning hours in a room provided by the general, expecting to get a few days off before being betrayed. Yes, Matthew knew betrayal was coming from the general. He had felt it just before leaving his meeting. It was a subconscious feeling the general was giving, picked up by the blade, that loose ends would be tied if trouble arose. Growing up in the Outer Ring made Matthew keenly aware that trouble always arose, it just happened much faster than Matthew wanted.

"I just wanted one good sleep in a bed like this. Was that too much to ask for?" Matthew cursed his luck as his blade sounded out the number that was coming to abduct him, ten soldiers with a captain making the eleventh. Matthew held his blade aloft and spoke at the item.

"Eleven is too many. Maybe if they were drunks in an alley, but trained soldiers with proper gears will chew through me. I need an exit." Matthew tried to remember the layout of the tower he was in. Forcing himself to find the stairs and exits in his mind. He knew of an exit beyond the soldiers that were inbound on his location, but other than that the tower was a mystery. He would have to push his way through the soldiers in order to escape. With little time to prepare, Matthew grabbed the blanket off of the bed and tied any object he could grab to the corners. As the soldiers approached the room, Matthew acted.

The door to the room swung open, and Matthew leapt out into the hall. With a quick motion he tossed the blanket at the approaching guards, but was dismayed as they cut his makeshift net out of the air and fired a couple of rounds at him. A jolt of lightning caught Matthew in the right leg, and he rolled around the corner of the doorway, back into the room. He could feel the soldiers' presence on the other side of the stone wall as he shut the door behind him.

"Alright little one, it's time to shine." Matthew whispered to his sword, and the blade hummed to life with a blue glow. He gave it a quick sweep to the right, building power into the blade, and thrust it at the wall where he felt a presence beyond. The blade slid through the stone as though it were water with the thrust, and Matthew quickly pulled the blade back to prevent it from getting lodged. The hole that remained, and the blood that filled it indicated the plan had worked, and a single soldier had been felled. "Just ten more and I might survive this." Despite his optimism, the soldiers on the opposite side had stepped back from the wall to avoid the reach of his gear. That trick would only work once.

"Surrender is your only option, we were sent to make an arrest not an execution." The Captain of this squad called out beyond the door. Matthew knew an execution is what he would get if he went out now and began building up power into the blade.

"Two swings from side to side and then a downward swipe." Matthew counted his motions as he swung, his blade colliding with the floor and leaving a clean cut. The door behind him let out a loud sound as lightning struck it, tearing it off the hinges and launching it towards Matthew.

"That's not normal." Matthew said aloud, surprised by the

intensity of this staff. Matthew pulled some of the blade's built up power into himself, coating his body in a light blue glow, and somersaulted over the incoming door, falling towards the floor blade first.

"Break through!" Matthew shout as he dispersed the remaining power from the blade onto the cut in the floor, shattering the ground beneath his feet and sending shrapnel in all directions. He landed on the floor below with a thud, knocking the air out of his lungs and forcing him to gasp in pain. With the power drained from his blade, Matthew was distinctly aware of the burning sensation that existed in his right leg.

"I need a bit more power." Matthew spoke softly to his blade and held it aloft, hoping to siphon some sort of emotional response to the shrapnel. The blade answered his plea with a faint blue tint and a numbing of his pain. Matthew jumped to his feet and sprinted from the room he had fallen into, narrowly turning a killing shot from a lightning staff into a graze across his left side and underarm.

The seared flesh hissed as he ran, but his own panic began powering the mysterious blade that he held. *I just have to make it to the street. Everything I've earned can be regained, I just have to survive this.* Matthew sprinted through the halls, guessing at the layout of the tower and prioritizing stairwells until he hit an impasse five floors above the ground level as his pursuers had caught up with him.

Fear and adrenaline pumped through Matthew's veins, pushing him towards the nearest room. Office or bedroom did not matter as Matthew kicked the door open. All he needed was.

"A window!" Matthew shouted in excitement as he rushed across the room, lightning striking just behind him. This particular shot caused alarm in Matthew, as it was the second shot fired with killing intent. Detainment was no longer an option. With this in mind, Matthew hurled himself out of the window from the fifth floor. In his mind, he could picture his blade hooking the windowsill, his feet planting onto the wall, and his body dropping one floor at a time until he was free. As his blade hooked the windowsill, a bolt struck him square in the back, with lightning tendrils pouring out from the front of his body. The shot cause his body to trip from the window and fall limp towards the ground.

A ring away from Matthew's fall, Debra, Beth, and Digit were quietly working their way towards the Inner Ring. To the three women, the destination was clear. They would have to make their way to Debra's father to present the ledger to the Judges.

"I just hope we are in time to do something about this." Debra fretted as the trio worked their way towards the innermost wall of Ebb. Debra was leading the way towards the gate.

"Wait. If we go towards the gate, won't we be captured?" Digit voiced her concern as they were approaching.

"It would be more obvious that we were up to something if we did not go straight towards the gate this early in the morning." Debra responded. "Besides, there is no way anyone would know what we did yet."

"Debra has a point. We should just make our way through the gate and towards her home." Beth agreed. Digit grasped her own palms together nervously, but continued on to the gate with her friends.

"Good Morning. A little early to be about aren't cha?" The guard at the gate greeted the trio in a friendly manner.

"Just looking about for early morning deals, sir." Debra called back.

"I'm going to have to ask you ladies for identification." The guard's words caused paranoia to begin building in Digit.

"Is ID now required to pass the rings?" Debra shot back, putting on an annoyed tone proper for a merchant's daughter.

"No ma'am, ID is not required for passage; however, the EAF is investigating suspicious people in the wake of a string of different incidents that have taken place around Ebb."

"And I am a suspicious person?" Debra replied.

"Y... No ma'am that is not what I am implying. I am merely complying with my superior officers." The guard responded. From the way he stood, the responses he gave, and the manner of speaking, Beth could tell he had not been on guard duty for long.

"Sir, I will present to you my identification as requested." Beth stepped forward and presented her military ID. Debra gave a slightly confused look at Beth's sudden interference but remained quiet.

"Ah, yes. Thank you." The guard took the ID and quietly began looking it over. He seemed to be evaluating some problem or process in his head as he thought hard about the ID presented.

"Will you not record that you checked my ID in the station log, sir?" Beth asked suddenly, snapping the man's attention away from the ID.

"Right, that is exactly what I intend to do with this." The man said and began walking towards the guard shack. Digit gave Beth a slight tug on her arm.

"He seems nervous." Digit whispered.

"I agree." Beth replied and approached the guard's shack. "First day of guard duty?" Beth questioned the man.

"Yes. This is my first day on this type of post." The man replied.

"We were all new once. As my ID states, I am Second Guard Elizabeth Warren. Nice to meet you." Beth held her hand out for a handshake.

"Nice to meet you as well. I am Rookie Mars Calvin." The man took her hand and gave it a quick shake. Beth gave a smile to the man in response.

"It is early, and my friend is in a hurry to get back to her shop before opening. Allow me to help you with the paperwork. You can ask your questions you need to ask us, and I'll fill this out for you. Then all you need to do is give it a proper review, and we are done." Beth stated and gave the man a moment to consider her offer before extending a hand to accept the log. The man hesitated briefly, but complied.

"Alright, I'll leave this to you and get my questioning done so we all can move on with our days. We will start with you ma'am." Mars directed Debra first. "You said your business this morning was looking for early specials. What type of business do you deal in?"

"My father, Mr. Bennet, deals in equipment for the Ebb Special Forces, and I work for him in acquiring designs from the gearsmiths in the Second Ring." Debra answered. The trio noticed the man visibly react to the word "Bennet" before getting back to his questioning.

"Is this an assignment given to you by Mr. Bennet?" The guard asked.

"Yes, it is a normal part of my regular job." The response seemed to be good enough for Mars, and he turned his attention towards Digit.

"And you, Identification and business." Digit looked concerned at the question. Being from the Outer Ring, she had no proper identification.

"Sir, I have already marked her identification in the log for you." Beth replied quickly, showing the entry in the log.

"Ah, thank you. Then give me your name and let me know what

you are doing out tonight."

"I call her Digit, and she carries my things for me, cleans my house, and manages my schedule like a good servant would. Please do not harass my help, as they are hard to find of good quality." Debra stepped in as well to assist Digit in the questioning.

"Thank you for the answer, but please allow her to speak for herself. How long have you been working for Miss Bennet?" Mars asked Digit.

"Six months." Digit answered the question quickly and quietly. To Digit, the man was moments away from asking her about her history of piracy, her involvement in the theft of the *Daisy*, and about her recent break in of the underground facility. She fidgeted nervously as the man stared blankly at her. She swore he recognized her. She knew he did and now he was going to call her out on her checkered past and…

"All right, you are free to carry on. Thank you for your time in keeping the city safe." Mars ushered the women on suddenly, as though an invisible alarm had went off inside his head. The sudden wrap up was accompanied by the sun beginning to rise over the horizon. The trio did not stop to consider what blessing had gotten them through the checkpoint, but instead rushed to get to Debra's house. Their decision quickly proved the wisest one, as soldiers suddenly took to the streets across the Inner Ring. The trio hid and watched as marching soldiers knocked on doors of judges and merchants, stabbing servants and arresting the families within.

The events on the street happened as such an accelerated rate, that only Beth noticed households being overlooked or bypassed. This was a targeted strike on the population. A culling of the disloyal. Beth stared with her standard stoic expression. Scanning the sudden crowd for information. She knew her life was safe today because of her recent injury. Had she been on duty, she too would have succumbed to a sudden attack or ambush. *I would not go down easy, but I would fall all the same.* Her expression held as she noted that there were very few judges being overlooked. This coup was between the merchants and the military. Beth turned her gaze to Debra.

Debra stood still, gripping the ledger tightly in her hands with a look of disgust and anger spreading across her features slowly. She knew she was too late. She could no longer look to the ledger and the wisdom of the judges to restore order in Ebb. There would be no judgment passed by those that were being marched out into the streets. Her actions this night were needed weeks or months ago, and the reality of the situation tore at her emotions. One major emotion held over all the rest, determination to survive this event and set things right. Debra turned to meet Beth's gaze. Each woman looked at the other, accepting their current fate and drawing strength from the other. An unspoken vow passed between the two women, and they turned to Digit.

Digit had hidden herself from view beside some trash cans. The other women found her easily due to the noise coming from her direction. Digit was letting out a soft sob that almost sounded like a squeak of a small animal. Her eyes were wide with terror and her body shook slightly. She had gripped herself into a tight hug as she focused on nothing. She was having a panic attack. Debra looked on with silent shock. She had seen Digit panic before, but had never seen it at this level. Beth approached Digit cautiously and slowly, so as not to surprise her. She then bent her tall frame and pulled Digit into a soft hug.

"I will not let them hurt you." Beth whispered softly to Digit, causing her gaze to meet Beth.

"We are here with you." Debra chimed in quietly, locking eyes with Digit. After a couple minutes, Digit pulled herself back to her feet, ready to move on.

"I'm sorry." Digit said, her voiced filled with sorrow.

"There is nothing for you to be sorry about. We are all scared." Debra reassured her. Morale restored, the women waited for an opening in the patrols and snuck through the Inner Ring towards Debra's home. The five minute walk from the gate took half an hour to accomplish, but the women finally arrived safely within the complex that had been left untouched by the marching soldiers, a fact that was not lost on Beth.

The building was a large two story villa with a detached store built beside it. The complex was outlined with a fence, and the women had to go through the store to get into the main complex due to the gates being locked tight. No sooner had the trio entered the main house when a booming voice called out to Debra.

"Thank goodness you are home safe."

FREEDOM BY CAPTIVITY

Debra, Beth, and Digit were hurried along by the short, stocky man into an inner room used as a study. Sweat dripped slightly down the man's face, displaying his clear nervousness as he stepped quickly past windows to prevent himself from seeing the horror taking place outside. The study was small compared to the rest of the house, an old nursery repurposed into a storage for entertainment, and contained a lining of bookshelves across the walls and a single violin on a stand. Two large chairs occupied the majority of the standing space, forcing the girls to huddle together for everyone to stand. Beth noticed that the windows in the room had been blocked a long time ago, making the only light source a large round gear that was nailed to the ceiling. The device gave off a faint blue light that barely lit the room, but quickly transitioned into a warmer and brighter coloration at the wave of the man's hand.

"There we are, safe and sound inside and away from all that nonsense happening outside." The man spoke to Debra alone, though he did glance at the other two women in a fashion similar to a patron glancing at animals in a zoo.

"Father, what is going on?" Debra spoke in a harsh tone, accusation evident in her tone.

"Whatever do you mean, pumpkin?" The man's voice shook slightly, years of doting on his only daughter had robbed him of authority.

"The soldiers on the street arresting judges." Debra pressed.

"I saw it from the windows, but I did not venture out to ask questions. A merchant that is too curious will quickly lose..."

"Their head. Yes, father. You've told me that one before." Debra cut him off. She could tell he was scared, but his fear was not of a man fearing arrest. His fear was a man's fear of meeting atonement. Debra slowly lifted the ledger into view for her father. Watching his eyes meet the book and then look away, as though he was refusing to acknowledge its presence. In this moment, Debra knew the author of the ledger.

"Father. Tell me what is happening. Help me understand this." She showed the book more forcibly in front of his face. His eyes trembled slightly before he spoke.

"It is what's best. It is best for the merchants and best for the town." He spoke slowly but with conviction. He did not merely say these words, he believed them.

"What's best? What's best! People are dying on the streets right now. Here in Ebb! In the Inner Ring!" Debra shouted suddenly, making her father draw back.

"Don't shout, dear. There is no need to attract attention to ourselves." The man whimpered, his eyes darting towards the door. Beth placed her hand on Debra's shoulder and locked eyes with her for a moment.

"I want to know the full extent of what is happening as well, but yelling might attract danger we do not need right now." Beth's responded to the situation before turning her attention back towards Debra's father.

"What's done is done, so there is no point in keeping it from you any longer." The man spoke quietly, "but you will need to keep your voices down. The world is messed up. The city is messed up, but General Sane is going to fix it. He called the major merchants together and discussed his plan for a coup. He didn't give all the details, but the major points was taking the judicial power out of the judges' hands and putting it back into the hands of the merchants. He told us we would not be subject to the whims of corrupt politicians fighting for power and handing down titles to family lines anymore. At first I figured he was a whacko, but then merchants started disappearing, and I realized how much power he already had. There was no turning against this event. There was no stopping it from happening. So I did what I had to."

"You helped him finance it?" Debra finished the thought for her father. His eyes shied away for a moment before he continued.

"Yes. I helped him find the financing for what he was doing. Gears, armor, weapons, food, soldiers. These things do not come freely, even for a General as powerful as Sane. I offered to run the books and get other merchants on board. This kept us from being a target, and puts us at the top of the new world that is being created. I knew people would be arrested, but I didn't know about the brutality of the event until I saw it. I can't speak up now, not until it is over. And you. You need to stay indoors for a while. I don't know how you got that ledger, but I know it would only bring you ruin if the soldiers found out about it. Best that you hand it over and show your friends to the guest rooms. It will be a bit of a long stay until things settle back into order." Debra's father finished his explanation with an extended hand. Debra stared at him dumbfounded. Cowardice and greed were all she could see in him. She turned her gaze away and looked to Beth and Digit for guidance and support. Digit gave her a quick nod, as she pressed balled up fists against the bottom of her mouth. Beth gave her the same stare that she had given her many times before, signaling her willingness to put her life on the line for whatever decision Debra made. Debra let out an exasperated sigh and handed over the ledger.

"Fine. For the present, I won't complain about the situation. Thank you, father." Debra gave a courtesy and waved her hand at her two friends, "if you will follow me to the bedrooms, please."

The women retired to different rooms, save from the chaos outside and thankful that they were at least trapped together during the transition and worried for Marla.

In the Second Ring, Marla had managed to bring Nathan safely to her workshop. She brought him in, under protest, and set him onto a chair to get a better look at his injuries. He was malnourished and thin, with a broken leg and many bruises. He had been abused quite heavily within the prison. As she looked him over, her eyes stopped on the gear that sat in his right eye socket. Its workmanship was incredible, but more so was the fact the prison guards let him keep it.

"We can't stay here. Your wings are a dead giveaway to this place. Only Alder would make something like those. While he might not be the most well-known gear smith in Ebb, at least a few of Richard's men will have heard of him and will be able to make the connection." Nathan cautioned while he was being checked over.

"Who would have even seen the wings to be able to tell about it? Besides, we can't go anywhere until I give you a means of supporting yourself." Marla responded while checking different parts on the wall. A few braces, a lift gear, and a small power pack typically used for the lighting gears the soldiers carry. Nathan was going to interject, but her work stopped him. He watched this young woman craft a new gear, her imagination being the only limit to her creation. He couldn't help but smile as an image of a younger Alder superimposed upon her. The same stance and posture, the same obsessive care, and the same drowning of logic preventing the creator from recognizing the situation they were in.

"You really were close to him weren't you?" Nathan spoke softly, almost to himself. Marla started fixing the brace onto Nathan's leg, a gentle look on her face.

"Yeah, he was a second father to me. He taught me more than just how to craft gears, he taught me how to live. He taught me to love the craft and treasure the art to it. He also taught me to use whatever is available, so that is what we are going to do." The brace now fixed onto Nathan's broken leg, Marla retreated upstairs while Nathan tried it out. The lift gear took the weight completely from the leg while the power pack made it take little effort to use. He would not be able to run or jump without pain, but walking was now possible, even in his current state.

"We are going to need to escape this town. I have some friends in a nearby farming village. They will hold us up for a bit while we figure out our next move, and I can train you on how to be a real gear mage in the process. We will just have to figure out how to get past the checkpoint. Your wings are looking fairly damaged, and I doubt they will last through another extended fight." Nathan called upstairs.

"They won't need too." Marla called back from the top of the stairs. She had dawned a red barrel shaped breastplate with a bird etched onto the torso. Her red hair had an unnatural glow to it, and in her hands she held fire. Her metal wings had changed to a light colored shade of red and her wing mail responded to the presence of Alder's fire mail. Nathan looked on with a slight smile.

The early morning troops stood at the southern gate towards the Outer Ring. Eight soldiers in total, far more than the standard two. They stood close by one another, huddled around the guard shack and watching for anyone foolish enough to ignore the message being blasted across Ebb. Watching for anyone to defy orders and walk out on the street at this time. They stood chatting quietly, laughing about a joke or the day's situation as Nathan approached. Even with the brace, he still had a visible limp. The soldiers turned towards him, two of them pointing lighting gears at him, the rest looking around for the obvious ambush this distraction was setting up. They didn't see anyone else, nor did they have time to fire upon the injured general before a large orb of fire struck down upon the crowd, instantly cooking the four in front before giving chase to the remaining four. In the sky above the soldiers, Marla was gliding down towards the ground in a circular fashion. The wings cried out in metallic groans as she taxed them again to get them into the air. On the ground she gave her hand a quick wave to lift the fallen metal feathers of the gear up and into a large bag full of equipment before turning towards Nathan.

"Good job. Now let's get out of here before anyone else shows up." Nathan spoke quickly. The duo exited the Second Ring and made a quick trip to the Outer Ring. With the light of day, and no reason to restrict the slums of the city, passing security on the gate only required a large sack fashioned into a cloak covering the gears. With one final look back at the Grand Market, Nathan and Marla escaped the city of Ebb and Richard Sane's grasp.

Matthew woke up weary and in pain. His wounds were treated, but he still felt the damage that had been dealt. He found himself laying in the back of a handcart between a couple of barrels and under a tarp. His sword was by his side, wrapped up tight to prevent the glow from being seen. The skyline he could see from his position showed no buildings of any sort, just open sky and daylight.

"How long have I been out?" Matthew asked his question to whomever was pulling the cart.

"'Bout half a day, I'd wager." The voice that greeted him was the familiar voice of Roger.

"Roger, you son of a dog. How'd you manage to pull me out of that mess?" Matthew collapsed back down into the makeshift bed Roger had put him onto.

"Well, I heard you calling out for help and then saw you trying to fly. I figured you were always bad at that and would likely need me to save you. So I did." Roger continued to pull the cart at a steady pace, away from the city of Ebb.

"So you did."

www.ingramcontent.com/pod-product-compliance
Lightning Source LLC
Chambersburg PA
CBHW020722160726
47993CB00006B/2308